Marie-Claire

Our CANADIAN *Girl*

Marie-Claire

KATHY STINSON

PUFFIN
CANADA

PUFFIN CANADA

Published by the Penguin Group

Penguin Group (Canada), 90 Eglinton Avenue East, Suite 700, Toronto, Ontario, Canada M4P 2Y3
(a division of Pearson Canada Inc.)

Penguin Group (USA) Inc., 375 Hudson Street, New York, New York 10014, U.S.A.
Penguin Books Ltd, 80 Strand, London WC2R 0RL, England
Penguin Ireland, 25 St Stephen's Green, Dublin 2, Ireland (a division of Penguin Books Ltd)
Penguin Group (Australia), 250 Camberwell Road, Camberwell, Victoria 3124, Australia
(a division of Pearson Australia Group Pty Ltd)
Penguin Books India Pvt Ltd, 11 Community Centre, Panchsheel Park, New Delhi – 110 017, India
Penguin Group (NZ), 67 Apollo Drive, Rosedale, North Shore 0632, New Zealand
(a division of Pearson New Zealand Ltd)
Penguin Books (South Africa) (Pty) Ltd, 24 Sturdee Avenue, Rosebank,
Johannesburg 2196, South Africa

Penguin Books Ltd, Registered Offices: 80 Strand, London WC2R 0RL, England

First published 2010

1 2 3 4 5 6 7 8 9 10 (WEB)

Marie Claire: Dark Spring copyright © Kathy Stinson, 2001
Marie Claire: A Season of Sorrow copyright © Kathy Stinson, 2002
Marie Claire: Visitors copyright © Kathy Stinson, 2003
Marie Claire: Angels in Winter copyright © Kathy Stinson, 2004

Design: Matthews Communications Design Inc.
Interior illustrations copyright © Sharif Tarabay
Map and chapter-opening illustrations (*A Season of Sorrow*) copyright © Sharon Matthews
Chapter-opening illustrations (*Angels in Winter*) copyright © Janet Wilson

Manufactured in Canada.

LIBRARY AND ARCHIVES CANADA CATALOGUING IN PUBLICATION

Stinson, Kathy
Marie-Claire / Kathy Stinson.

(Our Canadian girl)
A compilation of four previously published titles : Dark
spring, 2001; A season of sorrow, 2002; Visitors,
2003; and Angels in winter, 2004.
ISBN 978-0-14-317086-0

1. Montréal (Québec)—History—Juvenile fiction.
I. Title. II. Series: Our Canadian girl.

PS8587.T56M36 2010   jC813'.54   C2010-901626-2

Visit the Penguin Group (Canada) website at **www.penguin.ca**

Special and corporate bulk purchase rates available; please see
www.penguin.ca/corporatesales or call 1-800-810-3104, ext. 2477 or 2474

Dedicated with loving affection to some important twentieth- and twenty-first-century "Canadian Girls" in my life: my mother, Joyce Powell; my sister, Janet Barclay; my daughter, Kelly Stinson; my daughter-in-law, Antonella Stinson; my stepdaughters, Stephanie Carver and Kate Carver; and my granddaughter, Claire Tees. Also: Lois Gordon and Elspeth Latimer.

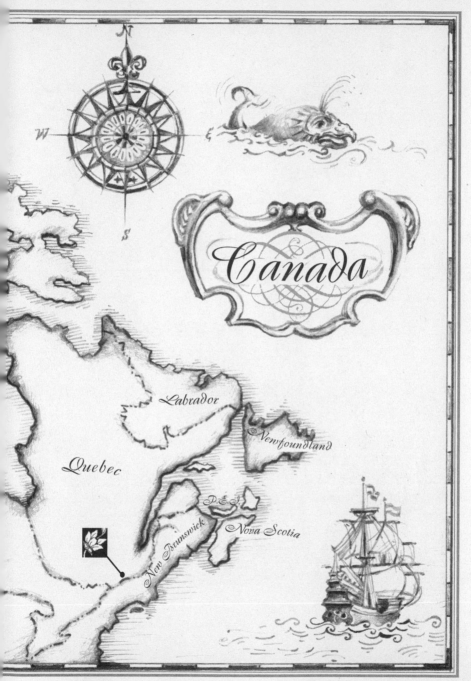

Canada

Labrador

Newfoundland

Quebec

P.E.I.

New Brunswick

Nova Scotia

 Marks the location of the story

Meet Marie-Claire

Marie-Claire is a French-Canadian girl living in Montreal.

In 1885, when Marie-Claire is ten years old, Montreal is one of the filthiest cities in North America. Garbage is not collected regularly. Untreated sewage contaminates the river and even the streets. Smoke from the growing number of factories pollutes the air. The stench of it all, especially during warm weather, is downright disgusting.

The adults in Marie-Claire's life understand that filth is in some way partly responsible for people getting sick so often, but the building of water and sewage systems cannot keep up with the needs of the city's rapidly growing population.

Many people, attracted by business opportunities and jobs for unskilled workers, have been coming to

Montreal from England, Scotland, Ireland, and from the Quebec countryside. Anglophones tend to settle in the west end of the city, francophones in the east.

Living conditions are worst for people like Marie-Claire's family, the working class which makes up the majority of Montreal's population. They cannot afford the fine stone homes at the base of the mountain. That's where business owners, bankers, doctors, and lawyers live. Marie-Claire's family lives closer to the river, where homes made of wood are crowded closely together and have no indoor plumbing—conditions ideal for the spread of disease. Diphtheria, cholera, tuberculosis, and smallpox have all visited the city in recent years.

Religion is an important part of most people's lives, including children like Marie-Claire. This is reflected in the way the steeples of Montreal's many fine churches stand out prominently against the city's skyline.

Wages are low, however, and working conditions unsafe. Taking care of a home and family is hard work. Both parents, and sometimes children, work long hours, six days a week. If even one parent is unable to work for any reason, the family's survival will depend on the resourcefulness and resilience of almost every family member.

This is the Montreal in which Marie-Claire lives in the "dark spring" of 1885.

BOOK ONE

Dark Spring

CHAPTER N° 1

Marie-Claire shivered in her thin nightgown. The kindling in the wood stove snapped. When the flame began to lick at the larger pieces of wood, Marie-Claire replaced the iron lid on top of the stove. Wouldn't Maman be pleased to wake up with the fire already lit? She was still so tired after Philippe's birth. Marie-Claire did not know just what had happened in her parents' room that day almost a week ago, but she'd heard enough to know that having a baby must be harder work even than churning butter or hauling water.

Marie-Claire crossed the cold floor to where Emilie still slept, curled beneath the grey blanket. How tempting it was to crawl back into the warm bed with her sister until the heat of the wood stove took the chill from the air. But if she wanted everything to be ready before Maman awoke, she must keep moving.

She slipped on her boots and wrapped her shawl around her shoulders before crouching beside the bed and pulling from under it the chamber pot. She carried it carefully so its contents wouldn't slosh out before she got downstairs to the privy in the lane behind their house.

Already a set of footprints in the snow led to the door of the little wooden shed. Marie-Claire could hear her neighbour grunting inside.

"Hurry up, Monsieur Flaubert. It's cold out here."

The door swung open. "Mind your tongue, you sassy little girl."

Marie-Claire scowled. She wasn't a little girl.

She was ten years old. Old enough to read and write and get up first and help Maman get the family ready for church.

She dumped her sister's nighttime urine down the hole, then lifted her nightgown and sat on the wooden seat, still warm from Monsieur Flaubert's big behind.

By the time Marie-Claire had emptied her parents' chamber pot, shaken the snow from her nightgown, hung it by the wood stove to dry, and got dressed, it was time to start breakfast. Marie-Claire put another stick of wood in the stove, poured water from the bucket into the kettle and set it on top. She cut five slices of bread from the loaf, ready to make toast—one piece for Emilie, one for Maman, two for Papa, and one for herself. Her baby brother was too little yet for more than the milk and water in his bottles, and her older brother had gone away with the army to help with a fight in the west. A fight with a man whose name—Louis—was the same as his own.

From the bedroom came a sudden cry. Papa

appeared in the doorway holding Philippe awkwardly in his arms.

"Here, Marie-Claire, you take him. Maman is getting dressed and I have to pay a visit."

Marie-Claire crooned a song to the baby as she danced him around the room. "*D'où viens-tu, bergère? D'où viens-tu?*"

"Marie-Claire," Maman said, "did you light the fire this morning? Such a helpful girl you are becoming. And look at this bread, already sliced. It will have to be thin ones for the rest of the day, though."

"I am sorry, Maman. I was not thinking of later." This being Sunday, the market, of course, would be closed.

"Never mind, *ma petite*. Let me feed Philippe while you go wake your sleepy sister. We do not want to be late for church."

CHAPTER N° 2

As they did every Sunday, as they had for as long as Marie-Claire could remember, her family met her cousin Lucille's family in the road and they walked together to the big church.

Except for the church bells, the streets were quiet that morning, the usual sounds of trotting horses, sleigh bells, and people calling to each other muffled by the heavy snow that had been falling all weekend. Wading through it, the women talked about the new baby and how little he slept between feedings. The men talked about how nice it was to sleep late this one day of the week when they did not have to go to work, although as a fireman Papa was sometimes called out no matter what day it was. As Emilie ran ahead with Lucille's little sister Bernadette, Marie-Claire and Lucille walked arm in arm, making plans for the future, when they would have big families of their own.

"Let's promise to live on the same street always," Lucille said.

Marie-Claire agreed. "That way we can do our laundry and take care of our children together, as my maman and yours do now."

Inside the church, the two families squeezed into their pews. The smell of wet wool and incense tickled Marie-Claire's nose in a pleasing way. The music from the organ sounded to Marie-Claire a little like crying, but it was a happy kind of crying, with her family—all except for Louis—kneeling together, elbows touching, thanking God for all their blessings. And Marie-Claire never tired of watching the hundreds of flickering candles while the priest preached the sermon and said prayers in his voice that was itself a little like music. "Please, God," he was saying, "accept today a special prayer for the well-being of our soldiers who have gone west to fight, and for an early end to the violence. Please, if it be part of your plan, bring these men home soon to their loving families."

"Oh, yes," Marie-Claire silently prayed, "please let Louis come home soon. Maman is worried about him, and Papa is worried too. I heard him say to my Oncle Henri that he does not like that Louis might have to fight against other French-speaking men. And I do miss him, dear Father, even if we do sometimes argue when he is helping me with my lessons."

Marie-Claire realized suddenly that everyone was standing. The organ was playing chords for the closing hymn. She rose quickly from her knees.

CHAPTER N.º 3

The snow continued to fall in fat flakes that clogged the streets. Going to school, Marie-Claire and Lucille carried their sisters on their backs, dumping them in huge drifts when they needed a rest.

The teacher, in her tidy black habit, a white wimple framing her stern face, scolded them in the doorway. "From the looks of your skirts, you have not been behaving as our Lord expects young ladies to behave."

"No, Sister," said Marie-Claire.

"We're sorry, Sister," said Lucille.

After school the girls thought nothing of how the Lord might expect them to behave. This was probably the last good snowfall of the season, and on the way home they ran and slid and jumped in the drifts. After checking that no adults were looking, Marie-Claire even threw a snowball at Jean-Paul, another of her cousins, who was on his way home from the boys' school.

"Let's build a snow fort," Lucille suggested.

In a great snowbank by the side of the road, Marie-Claire, Emilie, Lucille, and Bernadette dug and dug. Their fingers and toes were numb inside their thin gloves and boots, but in their dark little cave they giggled as they watched traffic go by, sleigh bells jingling from the horses' bellies as they pulled their carts and carriages through the heavy snow.

When one of the carts to go by was a fireman's hose wagon, Marie-Claire watched for the ladder wagon to follow. Where, she wondered, were the fire wagons going? Not to a house near where she lived, she hoped. So often, Papa had told her, when one house in a neighbourhood burned, so did others nearby.

But the ladder wagon did not come. Nor did a steam wagon. Perhaps the hose wagon was not on its way to a fire at all. It was odd that two firemen were riding in the wagon on top of the hoses.

A sudden unease gripped Marie-Claire. She crawled out of the snow fort into the street. The hose wagon was turning a corner—in the direction Marie-Claire lived. "Come, Emilie. We must go home. Hurry."

"Can't we play a little longer?"

"No. Come." Marie-Claire reached into the fort and yanked Emilie's sleeve.

"What is it?" Lucille said. "If you are worried your maman will be cross about your wet skirt, it is too late for that now."

"Something is wrong, Lucille. I know it."

Lucille and Bernadette ran to keep up with their cousins.

The fire wagon was parked in front of Marie-Claire's house, but the only smoke in the street came from chimneys. Marie-Claire ran up the stairs and, out of breath, pushed open the door.

The big shapes of two firemen filled the room. They were standing over Maman, who sat weeping in her chair. In Maman's hand a wooden spoon dripped gravy onto the floor.

Marie-Claire turned quickly to her sister. "You go with Lucille and Bernadette. I will come and get you later."

"What are those men doing here?" Emilie asked.

Marie-Claire pushed her sister out the door. "I will explain later."

In the cradle, Philippe was wailing. Marie-Claire picked him up to quiet him.

"Where is Papa?" She was afraid to ask, but had to know.

"Your papa is a brave man," one of the firemen said.

"I know that." Marie-Claire swallowed hard.

"But I asked you, where is he?"

"It was a very bad fire," the other fireman said, "up in Saint-Jean Baptiste village. A burning rafter fell, your papa could not get out of the way in time."

"He is dead?" Marie-Claire ran to Maman's side. "You are telling me Papa is dead!?"

"No, no, not dead. No." The fireman crouched down. Marie-Claire looked into his soot-streaked face. The smell of smoke was heavy in his woollen uniform. "But he is badly hurt. He will be in bed for some time. Your maman will need your help to take care of him."

Marie-Claire cradled Philippe in one arm. "My papa, may I see him?"

"He is sleeping," Maman said. "Don't wake him."

Marie-Claire peered into her parents' bedroom. Papa's face was soot-black. His neck and one cheek were red, blistered, and shiny where someone had applied grease. One arm, tied to a board with white bandage, lay on top of his blanket.

There were thick bandages around his shoulder, too.

How lucky they were, how lucky, that Papa had not been killed. Suddenly, in her wet clothes, Marie-Claire shivered. "Thank you, God," she whispered, "thank you. But please, if it is not too much trouble, while you are keeping Louis and the other soldiers safe out west, can you please help Papa to recover quickly?"

"Maman, what is all this?"

When Marie-Claire and Emilie came home from school, Maman was usually chopping cabbage or potatoes, stirring beans in the big pot on the stove, or going through the oats to take out mealworms before making porridge. Today, the wooden table was covered with piles of cut fabric. At a sewing machine, Maman was stitching two of them together.

"Shirts," Maman said. "At least they will be shirts when I have finished sewing them."

17

"So many?" Marie-Claire asked. Papa and Louis could not wear so many in a lifetime.

"Yes. Monsieur Grenier brings me the pieces that have been cut at the factory. He will bring more when these shirts are finished. Fortunately Tante Celine was able to lend me her sewing machine."

"You are working like poor Madame Masson up the road?"

"While Papa is unable to work. Yes." Maman's foot moved up and down on the pedal to keep the needle of the sewing machine moving as she spoke. "Will you get some onions from the pantry, please, and start chopping them?"

"How is Papa?" Marie-Claire found a corner of the table away from the shirt material and began to chop.

"Careful. Hold your fingers out straight. We don't want to find bits of them in the soup." Maman snipped the ends of thread from the seam she had just sewn. "Papa is in pain. It may be some weeks before he can get back to work.

While I am taking in sewing for Monsieur Grenier, I will need your help around here even more than before. I'm afraid you will have to miss school."

Marie-Claire hated the thought of missing school. The nuns were very strict, but Marie-Claire loved the arithmetic they were teaching— multiplying and dividing, much more complicated and fun than simple adding and subtracting.

Emilie tugged on the sleeve of Marie-Claire's dress. "Can you play with me?"

"Later, when I have finished making supper." But by the time Marie-Claire had finished chopping vegetables, fetched another bucket of water from the tap in the slushy back lane, set the soup on the stove, given Philippe a bottle, and taken Papa a mug of hot tea, it was time to help Maman clear the table of sewing. Supper was already late.

"Thank you, Lord, for the food you have provided," Maman said. "This is very good, Marie-Claire."

"Thank you."

"But a little more salt next time, eh?" With her fingers she took a pinch from the salt jug and sprinkled it in her bowl. "Tomorrow," Maman said, "we will need a bigger pot of soup. Your Tante Thérèse and Oncle Henri are coming."

"For supper?"

"Yes, and to live with us for a time."

"But where will they sleep?"

"Henri will sleep in Louis's bed. Thérèse will sleep with you and Emilie."

"Can't they just come for supper and then go back to their own house?"

"I cannot earn enough sewing shirts to make up for your papa's lost wages. Having your Tante Thérèse and Oncle Henri living with us will help us make ends meet. Also, as newlyweds, they are having trouble making rent payments. This will be a good arrangement for all of us."

"Maybe," Emilie suggested, "my Tante Thérèse can cook for us and take care of Philippe while you sew, so Marie-Claire can keep going to school."

"Thérèse cleans rooms at the hotel all day," Maman said, "while Henri works at the foundry. I'm sorry, Marie-Claire, if there was another way to manage . . ."

Some girls, Marie-Claire knew, were sent to live at the orphanage while their parents were having a difficult time. She would certainly rather give up school than do that. It was bad enough that Louis had to be away, but to be apart from her parents and from Emilie and Philippe, too? It was unthinkable.

Marie-Claire licked the last drip of soup from her spoon and brought the metal dishpan to the table. She lifted the square lid at the end of the wood stove.

"Oh, Maman. After I built up the fire, I forgot to fill the well with water."

"Don't worry," Maman said. "Let's just wash the dishes in cold water tonight. We're all tired." With grey circles under her eyes and her hair coming undone from its bun, Maman looked especially tired.

For a long time in the middle of the night, Maman was up with Philippe, trying to stop his crying. From her bed, Marie-Claire watched in the candlelight as Maman rocked him. She hoped he was all right. Their last baby, Pierre, had died when he was just a little older than Philippe. And the mess in Philippe's diapers lately was looking an awful lot like Pierre's did.

Marie-Claire slipped from beneath the blanket and knelt beside her bed for the second time that night. "Please, God," she whispered, "I love this baby so much. Please don't let Philippe die."

CHAPTER N.º 5

The streets were slushy and muddy, and as Marie-Claire hurried along, she had to jump over many large puddles. Ice on the river groaned. People were saying that if it jammed this year at breakup, there would surely be flooding.

With every puddle she jumped, Marie-Claire recited another multiplication fact. "Six times three is eighteen." During her absence from school she did not want to forget all she had learned. "Seven times four is twenty-eight."

She called "*Bonjour*" to the organ grinder on

the corner but could not stop today to talk. She had to fetch, before the store closed, more of the medicine that would stop Papa from crying out in his sleep. He got out of bed in the daytime now and did his best to be cheerful, but Marie-Claire could see in the tight muscles of his face that it took great effort.

In the square, not far from where she would buy the medicine, huge but shrinking lumps of ice were all that remained of the wonderful ice palace that had stood there during the winter carnival. What a sight it had been—the glassy walls glistening in the sun like giant diamonds, flags of France and England flapping snappily in the cold wind. Many times Marie-Claire and Lucille had admired the palace till their toes grew numb.

"Imagine being a servant in such a castle," Lucille had said.

"If you are going to imagine," Marie-Claire had answered, "why not imagine being the Snow Queen?"

How long ago that seemed now. How much

easier life had been then—before Louis went away, before Papa's accident, before Maman started sewing for Monsieur Grenier and Philippe was still safe inside her, when there was time for going to school and playing with Emilie and Lucille. Except for church on Sundays and the times Lucille came around with Tante Celine when she brought extra bread or soup, the girls had hardly seen each other at all since Papa's accident.

With the bottle of medicine now in her pocket, Marie-Claire longed to get on the streetcar, to sit on one of the wooden benches in the covered cart and let the horses pull her tired body closer to her home. But even with the wages of her aunt and uncle coming into the house, there were no extra nickels for streetcar fare. She would just have to pick her way as best she could around the garbage appearing in disgusting piles with the melting of the snow.

"It's terrible," her Tante Thérèse was saying when Marie-Claire entered the house, shaking mud from her skirt. "Just terrible. Their arms were swollen hard like big red balloons. And the fevers! You can't tell me this is better than smallpox."

"Whose arms?" Marie-Claire asked. "What fevers?"

"Marie-Claire, you're interrupting," Maman said, re-threading the needle on the sewing machine.

"It's all right, Hélène. At the orphanage—I heard about this at the hotel today, one of the cleaners there does some work for the nuns, too—at the orphanage, doctors came to give the children a needle. They say it's to keep them from getting *la picotte*, but you should see them. It's terrible. Me, I'd rather be sick than go through what those poor children . . ." Thérèse shook her head. "Apparently, a few people in the city are sick with smallpox and the doctors say it could spread. Sure it's bad, those ugly spots you get, but what's a few people? Do we know anyone who has it? No. What I know is, those needles they want to give are horrible."

"Will I have to get a needle, Maman?"

"Of course not. Be a dear now and see if Papa wants some of his medicine."

CHAPTER N.º 6

Huge slabs of ice cracked and heaved along the banks of the river. Warm winds rippled the surface of puddles, growing larger by the hour, in the streets and back lanes.

From his chair at the end of the table, where he was now able to sit comfortably for some hours, Papa said, "The noise of that river breaking up reminds me of artillery fire."

Marie-Claire placed a bowl of beans in front of him. "When I was down there yesterday, I could hear the river humming. *Humming,*

Papa, like it is something alive."

"It speaks, it moves, it rises and falls—who knows, maybe it *is* alive."

When the river flooded, its waters flowed over the harbour wall. They flowed on through the lower streets of the city where Marie-Claire and her family lived. The river water mixed with the filthy water draining down from the mountain. Water continued to rise till it covered sidewalks and seeped under doors.

Looking out the window, Papa said, "The family downstairs will be in it up to their ankles. We must invite them to come up here until the flooding recedes."

Marie-Claire's already crowded home became even more crowded as the grateful Flauberts dripped in carrying blankets and food. Monsieur Flaubert brought his fiddle, too. After supper that night the families sang and laughed together until Papa said, "I must get to bed."

Above the sound of Monsieur Flaubert's snoring, Marie-Claire heard Papa cry out sharply in his sleep, then Maman lighting a candle and rustling around for his medicine. "I am getting better," Papa whispered. "It is only at night . . ." Beside Marie-Claire her Tante Thérèse rolled over and mumbled something in her sleep. Emilie's hand reached up and stroked Marie-Claire's cheek.

On the floor, Monsieur Flaubert stopped snoring. His little boy said, "Is it morning yet?"

"Not yet, *chéri*," Madame Flaubert whispered. "Go back to sleep."

Marie-Claire closed her eyes. "Thank you, God, for keeping us all safe here, but please can you stop the flood by morning? Our house is really not big enough for all these extra people."

Outside, something thumped against the house. A chunk of wood maybe? Another dead cow? Was the spring flooding worse this year than last? Was God angry at the people of Montreal for something they had done or not done?

The next day, Marie-Claire hauled in extra buckets of water and boiled Philippe's diapers without complaining. She kept Emilie and the Flauberts' little boy entertained with stories. Muddy water continued to lap against the sides of the house. Except to visit the privy and the community tap, awash in flood water, no one ventured out.

By lunchtime they had eaten all the bread. Tante Thérèse suggested that she and Madame Flaubert could make some biscuits. Maman said, "Don't use any milk in them, please. Philippe will need what we have for his next bottle. The last one I gave him was mostly water."

Marie-Claire opened the window and leaned out. Could she see, above the muddy water, a wet line on the walls of the houses across the street? How much farther did the water have to fall before they could go out? She was about to close the window when, standing on some kind of raft, her cousin Jean-Paul appeared.

"Marie-Claire," he shouted, "is there anything I can bring your family?"

"Where did you get your raft?"

"The sidewalk on my street is busting up. I tied a couple of boards together, and *voilà!* Using another board for a paddle, I can go anywhere."

"Can you bring us some milk, Jean-Paul, for the baby?" She tossed down an earthenware bottle with some money in the bottom, which Jean-Paul caught neatly.

In twenty minutes he returned and tossed the bottle back up to the window. "Good catch, Marie-Claire," he said.

CHAPTER N.º 7

Finally, several days later, the Flaubert family returned home.

"Maman, I wish my Tante Thérèse and Oncle Henri would go home too." They were both out at work, so Marie-Claire could speak freely as she scraped the scales from the fish she was preparing for supper.

"We are lucky to have them here." Maman guided two pieces of material under the up-and-down needle of the sewing machine. "Without their help, I don't know what we

32

would do while Papa is unable to work."

"I could go to work at the tobacco factory," Marie-Claire suggested. "Josephine has a job there."

"Anyone who would hire such a young girl I do not want you working for. Besides, if you went away to work, who would help me here?"

"I can help you, Maman," Emilie said, rocking Philippe's cradle in the corner.

Maman was right, of course. Emilie could clean boots and help a little with the baby, but she could not do the work that was now Marie-Claire's—shopping, preparing meals for the family, hauling water for cooking, cleaning, and laundry. So many diapers she boiled every day. Also, even if she could take a paying job, as a child her wage would be very small.

"Maybe if I help you more," Marie-Claire said as she dumped fish guts into the slop bucket, "you can make even more shirts, and we won't need my Oncle Henri and Tante Thérèse any more."

Maman stopped the whirring machine. "Why do you want them to leave, Marie-Claire? I thought you liked them."

"I do. But beside me in bed my Tante Thérèse does not always smell very nice. And why does my Oncle Henri have to shout all the time? I am sure the Flauberts downstairs can hear every word he says."

"I'm afraid," Maman said, "that your Oncle Henri is losing his hearing. He does not realize he speaks so loudly."

"Losing his hearing? He is not much older than Louis, is he?"

"All the clanging and banging of machinery at the foundry twelve hours a day, six days a week— it is a wonder Henri can hear at all after two years working there."

Marie-Claire nodded. But still, she longed to have things at home back as they should be.

Before going to the market the next day, Marie-Claire slipped into the church to sit by herself in the quiet and remember what it had been like before the burning rafter crashed down on Papa. Sunlight shone in through the stained-glass windows.

"Please, God, help me be more patient with our crowded house, and don't let my Oncle Henri get any more deaf than he already is. Please can you try to mend Papa's shoulder a little faster? And please don't let my dear Lucille forget we are friends at this time when I cannot go to school or play with her." Afraid that asking so much would make her appear ungrateful, Marie-Claire added, "Thank you for keeping Philippe alive, even if he is still so sick, and thank you for getting Maman to say I don't have to get the awful needle that did bad things to the arms of the children at the orphanage."

On Sunday, with the candles flickering and the organ playing its sad but everything-will-be-all-right music, Marie-Claire bowed her head and said the same prayer. During the sermon, she leaned slightly forward and glanced along the pew to where Lucille sat, with her back straight and her hands folded in her lap. Lucille must have felt her friend's eyes upon her because she turned then toward Marie-Claire and smiled warmly.

"Let us pray," the priest said. He prayed that members of the congregation should choose the correct path, be grateful for their blessings, and honour God in their daily words and deeds. He prayed that the troops from Montreal should not be sent into the thick of the fighting in the west.

Marie-Claire was shocked to realize she had forgotten her big brother in her personal prayers. "Dear God," she quickly prayed, "forgive me for being selfish, please, and keep our Louis safe."

CHAPTER No 8

Day by day, as summer approached, the smell in the streets got worse. Barrels of manure overflowed into big puddles in laneways. Dead rats sprawled among rotting heaps of vegetable scraps, fish, eggs, and bones. One morning, between her home and the market, Marie-Claire counted six of them—and two dead pigs so disgustingly decayed that they must have been drowned in the floods earlier in the spring.

Around the market, where there were no privies at all, and where sewer drains were clogged with everything the butchers and other stall-keepers tossed out, Marie-Claire twice had to grasp her stomach and will its contents not to come up. With every step she took, something squished underfoot.

As she did the shopping, Marie-Claire did her best to remember all that Maman had taught her. Don't let anyone sell you meat that has maggots in it. The apple woman with the scar on her cheek has the nicest apples. Watch that the man selling flour does not put his finger on the scale. Don't ever pay for anything the first price you are given.

Marie-Claire roamed among barrels and baskets and carts, jostling against the other girls and women out to shop and catch up on the latest news and gossip.

"I hear the city hired a new scavenging company, cheaper than the old one, but are they doing *anything* to clean the streets?"

"He's bringing little enough money into that house and then he drinks most of it away."

"Can't you just smell the disease in all this filth? No wonder we've got smallpox in this city."

"But what would you have her do, Claudette?"

"Oh, I heard it is all over. A few cases there were. That is all."

"I hope so. A dreadful illness it is. If it doesn't kill you, its spots can leave you scarred for life."

"If you do get it, don't let the black wagon take you. In hospital you are almost sure to die."

With a cabbage, some carrots, and a few potatoes in her basket, Marie-Claire headed to a stall where chickens hung by their feet.

"How much for that one?" she asked. When the vendor reached up, she said, "I'm here to buy meat, not skin and bones. I was asking about the next one over."

The vendor placed the chicken on his scale. "Forty-five cents."

Marie-Claire wished she had enough money in her pocket to just pay it. She hated arguing for a better price. But Maman had said, "They don't expect you to pay what they ask." And it wasn't really arguing, it was bargaining.

Marie-Claire took a deep breath. "Not worth it," she said, and as Maman had taught her, she began to walk away. She hoped the next farmer would not be charging even more for his chickens.

"All right then, forty-one cents. Six cents off."

Marie-Claire turned back. "Six cents off makes thirty-nine." Holding herself tall, her heart pounding in her chest, she said, "I will pay you thirty-six."

The vendor handed Marie-Claire the chicken. "I am going to be a poor man at this rate."

"*Merci, monsieur*, thank you."

The man laughed as she headed off to buy a loaf of bread and a bag of beans.

With a few cents left in her pocket, Marie-Claire went to a stall inside the long marketplace and bought some beef bones. Sometimes a little broth in Philippe's bottle helped him sleep a little longer before waking again with his awful little cry.

Philippe stopped making the foul messes in his diaper. It seemed he was getting better. But one morning, after emptying the chamber pots, Marie-Claire realized that the house was oddly quiet. She ran to her parents' bedroom.

"I am sorry," Maman said. "Philippe passed away in the night. He was not strong enough."

"Why, Maman? Why wasn't he strong enough?" Tears streamed down Marie-Claire's cheeks.

Maman stared into the cradle. "It is God's way."

"But two babies in one family? It is not fair!"

Maman's lips almost disappeared in a thin line. "It is God's way."

Marie-Claire's bones felt heavy, but she tried to work fast that day so she could go to meet Lucille when she came out of school. She had to talk to someone who would understand how sad she felt. Maman seemed to have no heart left in her at all.

"But your maman is right," Lucille said. "It is not ours to question why God chooses those he does. And there are many babies God lets us keep for just a short while."

"That is all very easy for you to say. You have not had two babies die at your house before they had even one birthday."

"It is a shame your maman must spend so many hours sewing . . ."

"Are you saying it is *Maman's* fault that Philippe died? Or *mine*?! Lucille, you horrid witch! How can you be so cruel? You are as cruel as . . . as God!"

"Marie-Claire! You will be punished for saying such a thing. You had better hurry now to church and beg forgiveness."

"I will not! And I will never speak to you again! I wish instead of Philippe it was *you* who was dead!"

CHAPTER N° 10

Throngs of people packed the streets singing hymns. No one wanted to miss the parade for La Fête Dieu, winding its way, under golden banners and a hot sun, to Notre Dame. As crowds flocked into the vast church with twin towers, people agreed that this had been the grandest procession yet.

For Marie-Claire it was not. It was the only spring celebration of earthly blessings she had ever attended without Lucille.

In spite of the warm stuffiness of the church,

Emilie leaned against Marie-Claire in the crowded pew. Marie-Claire wrapped an arm around her little sister.

"Are you sad too?" she asked.

Emilie nodded. "Philippe never got to see a festival," she whispered.

"I know." If only Lucille understood.

All around, people's heads were bowed in prayer. Marie-Claire bowed her head too, but once again, like every day since Philippe's death, prayers would not come.

Coming out of the church, Marie-Claire and Lucille avoided each other's eyes, but Marie-Claire noticed how flushed her cousin's face was. Had it been that hot inside, or was Lucille ashamed of the cruel things she had said? Good. She should be. Or maybe she had a bad fever. That would be fine too.

Marie-Claire took Emilie's hand and Maman's arm and, without a word to Lucille, stepped into the street. She could not stop herself thinking such mean thoughts. Perhaps she was herself a bad person—fighting with her best friend, being glad if she had a fever. Being unable to think of something to thank God for was bad too, and the feeling she had that asking him for anything was pointless, because hadn't he let Philippe die, and wasn't Louis still out west, and wasn't Papa still unable to go back to work at the fire station?

Back home Emilie played quietly with her clothespin doll. Papa and Oncle Henri smoked their pipes while Tante Thérèse plucked a chicken and Maman chopped carrots. Maman never did her sewing on Sundays.

The pieces of fabric waiting to be sewn on Monday sat piled in the corner. Some of the pieces were quite small. About the right size, Marie-Claire thought, for a little dress for Emilie's naked doll.

Not wanting to interrupt the conversation Maman and her Tante Thérèse were having, she took one of the smallest pieces of fabric from the pile, threaded a needle and, wrapping the material around the neck of Emilie's doll, sewed her a dress. It was just a simple little dress, gathered around the neck and stitched down the back, but Emilie beamed.

Marie-Claire smiled. Maybe she wasn't such a bad person after all.

CHAPTER N° 11

The bishop was dead. Gathered round the table the day after La Fête Dieu, Marie-Claire's parents could talk of nothing else.

"We have so much because of him. Schools and hospitals, organizations to help the poor."

"Not to mention all the new churches."

"So beautiful . . ."

"He was a good man."

"A fine bishop."

But is death such a sad thing, Marie-Claire wondered, when someone is so old? There had been less talk about little Philippe, yet how much more her heart ached at his passing.

So much was the bishop loved that the procession for his funeral was even bigger than the parade for La Fête Dieu. Marie-Claire could hardly believe the hundreds of carriages and thousands of people in the streets. Among the faces were several, she noticed, covered in spots. Could these people have the smallpox her aunt and women in the market had spoken of? Were there now more than just a few cases of it in the city? Marie-Claire had only a moment to wonder before she was caught up again in the spectacle of bands, horses and carriages, bishops, police, students, nuns, and important men, all clutching prayer books or rosaries as they marched by.

Never before, Marie-Claire was sure, could the church have been so packed. Even when all the pews were filled, people continued to pour in the doors. From every pillar hung black-and-orange banners, like those hanging on many of the buildings outside.

Marie-Claire snuggled in close to Papa. It was wonderful to have him back at church. He had been exercising his arm and shoulder a lot and was able to sit and even stand for long periods now without having to go and lie down.

"A person would have to be dead himself," Papa said, "not to attend the funeral for such a great bishop as Ignace Bourget."

The chanting of the choir of hundreds echoed throughout the vast cathedral and hummed right through Marie-Claire's body. It put something back inside her, somehow, that had been missing. She bowed her head and thanked God at length for his many blessings, even for letting them have Philippe for a while. She thanked God for giving her back her ability to pray.

When she finished praying, she looked around for Lucille. She must be here today. Where was she? Marie-Claire wanted to go to her and tell her she forgave her the awful things she'd said and apologize for her own hurtful words. She found Lucille a few rows behind, between her parents, her head bowed. She would speak to her when the service was over.

When Lucille looked up, Marie-Claire's heart dropped into her stomach. Angry red spots covered Lucille's face. Some of the spots oozed shiny pus.

Smallpox? It must be. But had her Tante Thérèse or someone not said that people could die of this ugly thing? *Lucille, I wish you were dead.* That was what she, Marie-Claire, had said.

"Oh, dear God, please, no!"

"Marie-Claire, what is this?" Maman's voice cut like an axe into Marie-Claire's absent-minded stirring of the soup. "Did you do this?"

Maman held up Emilie's little doll, still proudly wearing the dress Marie-Claire had made. Maman's face was pulled into an angry scowl, angrier than Marie-Claire had ever before seen.

"I did, Maman. Emilie was so sad, I wanted to do something to make her feel a little better."

"And so you took something of mine without asking?"

"You were busy. It was just a little piece. I—"

"A whole shirt ruined because of *just a little piece.* You foolish, foolish child! Do you think Monsieur Grenier will pay me for a shirt that is missing a cuff?" Maman shouted. "No! He will charge me a fine for the ruined shirt! And after all the work I have done!"

"I am sorry, Maman, I truly am. I didn't know."

"As if things were not difficult enough!"

"I know, I know. I said I am sorry! What else can I do?!" Without waiting for an answer Marie-Claire ran from the house.

It wasn't fair. All she took was one little cuff! Was it her fault Maman worked for such a mean boss? Was that any reason to be so mean herself? It wasn't fair at all, when Marie-Claire worked so hard to cook, clean, take care of Emilie, do shopping and laundry, while all Maman did was sit around sewing shirts.

A hot, damp breeze blew off the river.

Of course, that wasn't true. Maman worked hard too. Marie-Claire had often seen her wince as she tried to stretch her back after so many hours bent over the sewing machine. And now, because of her awful daughter, Maman would not get all the money she had earned.

Everything, it seemed, was because of her, Marie-Claire. Maman being upset, and the family being short of money. The fact that her cousin Lucille was sick and dying was her fault too. Marie-Claire ran and ran, but she could not get away from herself.

At the market, with a stitch in her side and sweat pouring down her forehead, she trudged aimlessly from stall to stall. Tonight before bed she would pray for a good long time. She would ask God to help her be a better person. In the meantime—yes, she had a little change in her pocket left over from the trip to market when she had got such a good bargain on a block of cheese. Was it enough to buy a loaf of the bread Maman especially liked but bought only for special occasions? It would not make up for the ruined shirt, and maybe Maman would be angry if she spent money on bread unnecessarily, but Marie-Claire wanted so much to make some kind of peace offering.

Luck was with her. The bread was a day old and she got it at a very good price. Quickly she made her way toward home, her dress sticking to her back.

"Marie-Claire! Come!" Jean-Paul shouted. "On your street! The black wagon!"

Marie-Claire hugged the loaf of bread she had bought and ran behind Jean-Paul to the end of the dirt lane where she lived. Outside Lucille's house was parked the black wagon. Policemen were shouting at Lucille's father.

"She must go!"

"No. Please!" Lucille's father begged. "We can take good care of her at home." Behind him cowered Lucille, tears streaming down her spotty face.

Marie-Claire had heard that people with *la picotte* were sometimes forced to go in the black wagon to the hospital, but her best friend? "This is not possible," she whispered. She must go to Lucille right now and beg her forgiveness. She must pray to God to correct this awful mistake.

But before she could get near Lucille, the doors of the black wagon, with Lucille inside, slammed shut.

CHAPTER N°13

Throughout all the singing and speeches on Saint-Jean Baptiste Day celebrating the survival of the French-Canadian people, Marie-Claire could think of and hope for the survival of just one of them. "Lucille, Lucille, you must get well."

So that her Tante Celine could go and visit at the hospital, Marie-Claire offered to take care of Lucille's little sister. She took Bernadette and Emilie down to the river to watch the men in shirt sleeves loading big sacks, barrels, and boxes onto the huge ships. When the girls tired of that,

Marie-Claire tied a rope to a lamppost and turned it and turned it till finally the girls grew tired of skipping, too. At home, she worked fast and hard as if, if she could just be good enough, it would help ensure Lucille's recovery. "And please, God," she prayed, "can you try to prevent the spots from leaving permanent scars? Lucille has such a pretty face."

When, two weeks later, Marie-Claire heard that Lucille was home, she whooped with joy.

"Please, Maman, may I go and see her?"

"Of course. Go. You have been working your fingers to the bone here. You'll be an old woman before you're twelve years old at the rate you've been going. Go now. I'm sure Lucille will be pleased to see you."

Will she? As Marie-Claire passed the scavengers shovelling slimy garbage into wagons, she wondered.

"Come in, Marie-Claire, come in." Her Tante Celine was up to her elbows in flour. "Lucille is just picking over the oatmeal for me. It's so good to have her home again."

Lucille's head was bent over a sack on a chair in front of her. With her fingers she gently sifted the oats, pausing occasionally to toss a mealworm into the fire.

As if sensing something between the girls, Tante Celine suddenly wiped her hands on her apron, said, "I just remembered something I must be doing," and left them alone.

"Lucille, I came to apologize," Marie-Claire said quickly. "I am sorry for what I said." When Lucille said nothing, Marie-Claire went on. "I cannot stand it when we argue. I said things I did not mean and I was so afraid—oh, Lucille, you don't know how afraid I have been. When you went to hospital I thought you would die and it would be all my fault."

"Do you really think you are as powerful as all that?" Lucille looked up at Marie-Claire for the first time. Faded spots still marked her forehead and one cheek. "And do you honestly think you were more frightened than I?"

"No. Of course not. No. But please, Lucille . . ." Marie-Claire pulled a chair over beside her cousin and sat down. "Can you please try to find it in your heart to forgive me?"

"Marie-Claire, can you imagine being in hospital, your throat parched and your ugly skin burning up and no one comes for hours with a glass of water or a cool cloth? Can you imagine lying there and beside you in the next bed a girl has died and you call for the nuns to come, but there are so many patients, who knows when they will?"

Marie-Claire let her tears drop into her lap. After all Lucille had been through, it was no wonder she could not forgive her.

"But it is not your fault I got smallpox," Lucille continued. "It is not your fault I went to hospital. There are so many people in the city with the disease now, they are saying it is an epidemic. And of course . . ." Lucille smiled then, "of course I *must* forgive you. I could not bear it either when we were not speaking."

Marie-Claire pushed the oatmeal bag out of

the way, threw her arms around her cousin, and kissed her on both cheeks. Her face must have betrayed what suddenly occurred to her, because Lucille laughed and said, "Don't worry. They would not have sent me home if I were still contagious."

"To be honest, Lucille, I would be more worried if we could not be friends again than I ever could be about getting sick."

"We *are* friends again." Lucille grabbed Marie-Claire's hands and squeezed. "We are friends now, and we will be friends forever."

Papa stood in the middle of the room wearing only an undershirt and trousers. In each hand he held an iron pot. With his arms stretched to either side, he slowly lifted the pots up and over his head. Slowly he lowered them again to his sides.

"Josèph, it is wonderful how well you are getting back your strength," Maman said, "but isn't that enough for today?"

"Nonsense," Papa said. "Put some potatoes in these pots so I can work these muscles harder."

"I'll work those muscles for you," Oncle Henri suggested, rolling up his sleeves. "Come on, Josèph. How about it?"

Papa set down the pots and faced Oncle Henri across the table. "Ready?"

Elbows braced on the table, the men locked hands.

"Go."

Each man tried to push the other's hand down flat to the table. Blood vessels stood out on the backs of their clenched fists. Raised knots of muscles in their arms and across their shoulders quivered. Marie-Claire clenched her own fists, as if doing so would add to Papa's strength.

After a long minute, sweat shone on Papa's face, his arm began to tremble, and Oncle Henri was able to push Papa's hand a little closer to the table. Grunting, Papa pushed back. When the two clenched hands were again upright, Marie-Claire and Emilie cheered. Oncle Henri eventually got Papa's arm down to the table, but still the girls cheered. Papa was getting so much stronger.

In time he was strong enough to carry hoses, buckets of water, even another man if necessary. The day he returned to work, Marie-Claire put extra chunks of ham in his beans and packed an extra-thick slice of bread and butter in his lunch box.

When Monsieur Grenier came to pick up Mama's shirts and bring her more pieces to sew, Mama said, "Bring me only half this number next week. My husband is back at work now. And I must get back to my work here at home so my daughter can get back to school."

At the end of the room, where she was scrubbing the floor, Marie-Claire smiled.

That night, after the family had given thanks for the food they were about to eat, Oncle Henri announced in his big voice, "Thérèse and I will soon be leaving you."

"Why?" Maman asked.

"Where will you go?"

"You don't need us here any more," Thérèse said, "and I heard at the hotel that the men we sent out west are on their way home. Riel has fled, and the rebellion is over."

Marie-Claire dropped her fork to her plate. "Our Louis is coming home?"

"If it be God's will," Maman said, her voice full of hope.

"Oh, please, God, let it be so," Marie-Claire exclaimed. "But, my Tante Thérèse, do you and my Oncle Henri have to go? We can make room here for everyone."

Maman smiled, then looked to Thérèse and Henri. "Perhaps your aunt and uncle have other reasons to be finding a home of their own?"

"We are going to go to Toronto," Oncle Henri said. "I hear they pay men a decent wage there."

"But, Henri, you will not find many French people in Toronto," Papa said.

"My English is pretty good," Henri said. "We will be all right."

The festive mood at the table seemed broken by this news. Everyone was chewing quietly when Tante Thérèse spoke again. "Also, when winter comes, our household will have an additional little member."

"We are getting a dog?" Oncle Henri teased. "You didn't tell me!"

Tante Thérèse laughed. "If Henri finds a good enough job, we will all be able to come on the train to visit you here at Christmas."

Such a long time away Christmas seemed now, with the suffocating heat of summer wrapped tight round them.

"Let us give thanks," Papa said, "for your good fortune."

"And for the hope that Louis may be home soon," Marie-Claire added.

"And for Josèph's recovery," said Maman.

"For all the good things in life," Oncle Henri shouted, "let us say *merci infiniment!*"

Together everyone at the table said, "Amen."

BOOK TWO

A Season
of Sorrow

CHAPTER N° 1

Marie-Claire pounded dirt from the braided rug hanging over the clothesline behind her home. Sweat trickled down her face and back. Her shoulder muscles ached. She leaned over the railing into the laneway and sneezed.

When she dragged the rug back inside to the freshly swept floor, Maman looked up from her work.

"There is a little extra money this week," she said. "Why don't you and Lucille take this and go to the circus? You deserve it, after all your hard work." Maman handed Marie-Claire two coins and began again to pump the pedal of the sewing machine.

"*Merci*," Marie-Claire said, "but are you not coming, too?"

"I don't need a circus." Maman folded another finished shirt and placed it on the pile. "I need only to have my family back together under one roof."

"Papa says that with what is happening in the West, Louis may be home soon."

"I pray each night this will be so." Maman coughed. "You girls go now. I must sew one more shirt before Monsieur Grenier comes from the factory to pick up the next batch."

"I hope you will at least stop for a cup of tea first," Marie-Claire said. "*Au revoir*, Maman."

All the way to the circus grounds, Marie-Claire and her cousin chatted happily, oblivious to the smells from the slaughterhouses they passed, the barrels of decaying fish, the rotting fruits and vegetables in the markets, and the manure on fire at the city dump. On three houses in one street, sanitary police were putting up the black-and-yellow placards that told everyone that someone living there had smallpox.

"See my spots, Marie-Claire?" Lucille said. "They are almost gone now."

"Yes, you are looking much better." Lucille's spots were certainly fainter than they had been when she had smallpox in the spring, but Maman had said they might never fade completely.

Above the entrances to the circus tents, illustrated posters lured visitors to come inside—posters for John Coffey "The Ohio Skeleton," Krao the Missing Link, and Chang the Famous Chinese Giant.

Marie-Claire clung to Lucille's sleeve so as not to lose her in the crowd. "What shall we go to see first?"

"I hear the giant is very handsome."

The girls pushed their way to the front of a crowd.

"*Mon Dieu!*" Lucille exclaimed. "He must be over eight feet tall."

Marie-Claire pulled Lucille away, behind others gawking at the giant.

"What is it?" Lucille asked. "Do you not think he is lovely?"

"He smiled at me," Marie-Claire said, blushing. "Let's go."

At the next exhibit, Lucille said, "Why, that must be the skinniest man in the world."

"You can almost see his bones beneath his skin."

On the other side of the huge tent, the girls stared at a man who looked as much like an ape as a human being.

Outside again, the sun beat down hard upon their heads.

"Lucille, do you mind if we find somewhere to sit down for a minute?"

"What's wrong?"

"My head . . ." Marie-Claire held it between the palms of her hands as Lucille led her to the shade of a circus tent. "And I feel so terribly hot."

"Oh, Marie-Claire, this is how . . ."

"How what?"

Lucille shook her head. "Nothing. I am sure it is nothing."

"I know what you were going to say." Marie-Claire felt suddenly hotter. "You were going to say this is how smallpox begins, weren't you?"

"Before my spots came I had a bad fever and the very worst headache," Lucille admitted. "But does your back hurt, too?"

"No."

"Then I am sure you are just suffering from the heat."

Beside a circus tent Marie-Claire lowered herself to the dusty ground. "Oh, I do hope so, Lucille."

Lucille put a protective arm around her cousin. "I hope so, too."

"Today *is* a very hot day."

"Yes, very hot," Lucille agreed.

"But I have had enough of the circus. Can we go home now?"

As much as possible the girls kept in the shade of buildings as they made their way slowly through the streets. On many houses, tattered remains of placards hung listlessly in the heat. Above them, smoke from the city's factories, hospitals, and manure fires continued to drift across the sky.

At home Marie-Claire gulped tepid water from the bucket beside the wood stove. The bucket was almost empty. Her head still pounding, she plodded downstairs to the tap in the laneway, refilled it, and hauled it back upstairs into the stifling house.

"It is so hot," Marie-Claire said. "Shall we just have some bread and cheese tonight?"

At the sewing machine Maman coughed. "Papa may be hungry when he gets home if there have been many fires to fight today."

But when Papa came home, he said no, there had been only two small fires, and the men of his station were not called. He had spent the day dampening down dusty streets. "I wished I was one of the little boys," he said, "running along behind the hose wagon, soaking myself in the spray."

Marie-Claire laughed to think of Papa doing such a thing, and realized her headache was gone and she no longer felt feverish.

After their small supper, the family went outside to sit on the iron steps where the air was a little cooler. Maman coughed again as she sat down.

"Are you not well, Hélène?" Papa asked.

"I am fine," she said. "It is just the smoke from that manure fire. Can nothing be done to put it out?"

"I am afraid not. All we can do is wait. It will burn itself out in time."

A horn from a distant freighter on the river sounded. From a street nearby came the angry voices of a man and a woman shouting. In a house on the other side of the lane a baby cried.

How little Philippe would have hated this heat, Marie-Claire thought. But how she still missed her baby brother's presence in their home.

"Come, Emilie. Sit on my lap."

Marie-Claire's sister climbed onto her lap. "Are you going to tell me a story?"

"What kind of story would you like to hear?"

"A story about an angel."

Marie-Claire had barely begun her story when Maman stood up and said, "Sweet Jesus, am I to believe my eyes?"

CHAPTER N.º 2

Approaching through the grey dusk was a tall young man in a tattered soldier's uniform. Maman and the rest of the family hurried down the stairs to meet him.

"Louis, you are home!" Maman said. "At last, you are home!" She stood on tiptoe and kissed him on both cheeks.

For almost four months Marie-Claire had been missing her big brother. Now she felt suddenly shy. But after Louis hugged Maman and shook hands with Papa, he gathered Marie-Claire and

Emilie in his arms. Immediately, Marie-Claire's shyness disappeared. As soon as he was settled on the steps with a cold drink, she insisted on sitting with Emilie on Louis's knee.

When the girls finally had their fill of big-brother tickles and singing, Papa said, "Tell me, son. Was the fighting in the West very bad?"

Louis sighed.

"Perhaps you should wait till the women have gone to bed to talk."

"There is no need." Louis tipped the bottle to his lips. "Les Carabiniers Mont-Royal were not, in the end, sent into the thick of the fighting."

"That is good," Papa said. "French men should not have to fight other French men."

Across the lane a baby continued to cry.

"I am so glad you are home, Louis," Maman said, dabbing her eyes with her sleeve.

"So am I," Louis said, "so am I. But I hear we soldiers are now to do duty as sanitary police. Tell me, what is happening here in Montreal?"

Just then, Emilie yawned a noisy yawn.

"Come along to bed, Emilie," Marie-Claire said.

"Will you finish the story about the angel?"

That night Marie-Claire lay awake for a long time trying to get comfortable. Beside her, Emilie's hot little body sprawled over more than her share of the bed. Even after Louis was snoring in his bed across the room, and after her parents had finished saying the rosary in those hypnotic voices that usually put her to sleep, Marie-Claire was wide awake and so awfully warm. If I try to lie perfectly still, she thought, can I perhaps fool myself into falling asleep?

Through the wall between their beds, she heard Papa speak.

"They want all the men at the fire station to get it, this vaccination. They say the children should have it, too."

Maman said, "It made children sick at the orphanage. Remember Thérèse telling us about their swollen arms and fevers? Poor dears."

"But the smallpox . . . People are dying. Claude at work has lost both his children. Doctors are saying that if you get the needle you never have to worry about smallpox again."

"Yes, but I read in the paper that other doctors say vaccinating people is only helping to spread the disease. Whom are we to believe?"

"I don't know, Hélène, I don't know . . ."

Marie-Claire tried to imagine one of Maman's sewing needles sticking into her arm. Ouch! She wanted nothing of it.

"What they do, I understand," Papa continued, "is they inject into your blood the germs from a sick cow."

"And this is supposed to keep you from getting the smallpox? *C'est ridicule.*"

"Some of the papers are calling it an epidemic."

"But it is nothing like what happened in the seventies, eh?"

"I hope not. That was a bad epidemic, that one . . ."

It was a long time before either of her parents spoke again. Marie-Claire thought they had gone to sleep.

"You know," Papa said, "they are building an addition to the smallpox hospital."

"Maybe it is worse than we think."

"Maybe."

"Why has it come again, do you think, Josèph—*la picotte*?"

"Some say it has been sent as punishment for the carnival last winter," Papa said. "All that worldly festivity without a thought to God and the Church . . ."

Marie-Claire sat upright in her bed. Punishment for the winter carnival? She loved the winter carnival, the excitement of seeing people hurtling down the toboggan runs, and especially that magical ice palace in the square. Just thinking about it made her feel cooler. And she could not believe God would want to punish anyone for something so beautiful.

"Others say," Papa went on, "it is because the city is in such a state of filth."

"I suppose," Maman said, "only God knows why it has come."

"And what it will take to make it go."

"I think I would like to pray some more before I sleep," Maman said.

"I love you, Hélène."

Marie-Claire heard the rustling of her parents' bedclothes as they got to their knees beside their bed. To the sound of their prayers, and still thinking of the ice palace glistening in the bright winter sun, she finally fell asleep.

CHAPTER N° 3

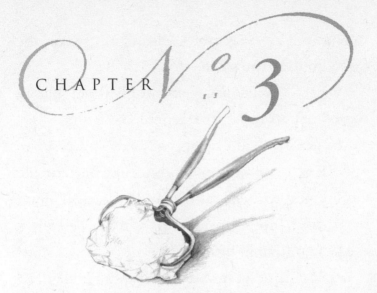

The next morning, Marie-Claire did not wake until Papa was about to leave for the fire station. She lifted her head from her pillow. Emilie was already finished her toast and Maman had biscuits in the oven.

Passing by, Louis tousled Marie-Claire's already messy hair. "Aren't you the little sleepyhead," he said. "Is this what you have been doing while I have been gone?"

"Don't you think that for a minute," Maman said. "Your sister has been working very hard. She can now chop vegetables, clean fish, sweep the floor, go to the market—"

"Whoa!" Louis laughed. "Off I go, before someone puts me to work here."

Marie-Claire rolled out of bed, and Maman said, "It is a good thing Tante Celine and Lucille are coming to help with laundry today. I don't think your brother's uniform was washed once the whole time he was away."

Marie-Claire visited the privy and changed out of her nightgown. Although the house was already very warm, she added two more sticks of wood to the fire in the stove, and from the back lane began hauling buckets of water to fill the big wash kettle. She stripped the sheets from the beds and put them in to soak. Soon Lucille, Bernadette, and Tante Celine arrived at the door.

Emilie and Bernadette, too little to help with laundry, skipped off to the end of the room to play quietly with their clothespin dolls.

Steam rose from the wash kettle on the wood stove. Maman pushed the long wooden laundry stick back and forth through the hot soapy water, through the heavy clothes and bedding. She, Tante Celine, Marie-Claire, and Lucille took turns pushing back and forth till the water was almost black, back and forth till their shoulders ached.

After fishing the wet things into an empty kettle on the floor, Maman and Tante Celine together carried the large kettle of dirty water outside.

"Watch out below!" Maman called. Into the laneway cascaded the scummy grey wash water.

Marie-Claire and Lucille trudged down to the tap shared by all the families whose homes backed onto the lane. Down and up, down and up, fetching buckets of clean water for rinsing.

"Look at you," Lucille said. "It is hard to say if you are more soaked with sweat or with wash water."

Marie-Claire sighed. "And still there is all the wringing to do."

"Let's do it outside," Lucille suggested. "At least there is a little breeze there."

One girl on either end of a pair of Papa's heavy work pants, they twisted and twisted till no more water dribbled out of them. While Maman and Tante Celine wrung the bedding and hung it on the line, Marie-Claire and Lucille wrung out the clean clothing for both families, one piece at a time.

"I am not sure it was wise to wash Louis's uniform," Marie-Claire said. "It is now almost completely in tatters."

"Never mind," Maman said. "I will be happy to rip it up for rags."

When all the laundry was hung, Maman coughed. "So much water on the floor," she said, "I may as well wash it now."

From the window Emilie called, "The ice wagon!"

Together, she, Bernadette, Lucille, and Marie-Claire clattered down the stairs. They hurried to catch up with a group of children running along behind a slow-moving wagon. When it stopped, the iceman lifted the blanket and took down a big block of ice—big enough to keep an icebox and all the food inside it cold for several days. With his heavy tongs he carried it to someone's house.

While he was making his delivery and collecting payment, all the children grabbed chips of ice from the wagon. They rubbed them all over their hot faces and necks. As soon as they saw the iceman returning, they each grabbed one last chunk and ran.

Marie-Claire, Lucille, and their little sisters strolled home along the wooden sidewalk, drinking up the cool wet drips of melting ice.

CHAPTER N.º 4

Finally the day came for school to start again. So long it had been since Marie-Claire had been able to go. She could hardly bear to take time for breakfast.

"Drink your milk, Marie-Claire," Maman insisted. "It is good for you."

She had missed months of school when Papa was off work with his burns and a broken arm, and then it had been summer. Would she remember the arithmetic she used to be so good at after all this time? Marie-Claire got

Louis to drill her on her three-times table as she forced her milk down in little mouthfuls.

As she and Lucille skipped to school, their eyes watered with the nasty smells of sewage and of disinfectants sprinkled through the streets to try to keep the smallpox under control. At one corner, the girls stopped to let a black wagon go by. The crying face in the window was an ugly mass of oozing spots.

"Lucille," Marie-Claire asked, "that wasn't Eveline, was it?"

"Eveline?"

"You know. The girl from school who does so well with memory work?"

"I think you may be right," Lucille said. "So clever she is. I do hope she doesn't die."

"Many who are taken to the hospital do, my Tante Thérèse said."

"It is a vile place," Lucille said. "I pray that you will never have to go there."

Marie-Claire giant-stepped over a heap of something slimy, and Lucille followed.

There were fewer girls at school than Marie-Claire had expected to see. Last year the class-room had been so crowded that on some days there were not enough chairs for everyone, and some girls had to sit on the floor. Today several chairs sat empty.

After opening prayers, Sister Ernestine asked, "Does anyone here at school today have someone at home with smallpox?"

The girl beside Marie-Claire raised her hand.

"I am afraid," Sister Ernestine said, "that I am going to have to send you home."

"I do not have *la picotte* myself," the girl said, "just my sister. She stayed home."

"That is good," Sister Ernestine said, "but the priest has said that children with any smallpox at home must not come to school. I am sorry, Micheline. I know what a good student you are. I hope your sister gets well soon."

After school Marie-Claire stopped by the market to buy some fish and cabbage. Although Maman was not working so desperately hard sewing shirts now that Papa was able to work again, she still needed Marie-Claire to do some of the shopping, and often to cook supper.

Leaving the market, Marie-Claire saw a man get on a streetcar with a package. A moment later he got off, complaining to anyone who would listen, "Says no passengers with parcels allowed. What does he think? That I'm carrying a bag of smallpox? For mercy's sake, it is a bag of flour!"

When Marie-Claire was almost home, a hearse passed by, a yellow flag at its window. Marie-Claire shivered. Yet another person dead from this awful sickness.

Marie-Claire was cleaning fish for supper, poking the knife behind the gills, when there was a knock on the door.

"Will you get that, Emilie?" Maman said. "Your sister's hands are dirty and I want to get this shirt finished before Papa gets home."

Emilie led two men into the house. One of them carried a black bag. "Good afternoon," he said to Maman. He spoke loudly and slowly. "You have no doubt heard about the wonderful vaccine that can prevent the dreadful smallpox?"

Maman stopped pumping the foot treadle on the sewing machine and stood up. "I have."

"In the interests of stopping the epidemic, we are here to give vaccinations to your children."

The knife in Marie-Claire's hand slipped on the slimy fish.

"Thank you," Maman said. "We do not wish to vaccinate."

"But the disease is killing more people in the city every week as the summer progresses, Madame." The man glanced around the small, sparely furnished room. "And the vaccination is free."

Maman's spine straightened. "I said, we do not wish to vaccinate."

Marie-Claire squeezed her nicked finger in her apron.

"Such beautiful girls you have," the other man said, and smiled. Marie-Claire could see it was not a true smile. "It would be a shame to see their lovely faces marked—"

"My husband and I choose to let God spare our children—or not—as is His will."

The man opened his mouth to speak again, but Maman said sharply, "Good day, gentlemen."

"Oh, Maman," Marie-Claire said when they were gone, "I was afraid when you said 'thank you' that you were going to let them do it."

"I told you the day your Tante Thérèse came home with the awful story of the children at the orphanage that I would not. I do not go back on my word."

"I know you don't, Maman. And I would certainly much rather trust in God than in either of those dreadful men."

"Such beautiful *gir-r-ls*." Emilie giggled at her imitation of the awful English man Maman had sent away.

"Go and wash up for supper now," Maman said. "Papa and Louis will be home soon."

That night in bed, Marie-Claire heard Maman pray, "Please, God, let that be the right thing to have done today—sending away those men with their needles."

CHAPTER N°5

On Sunday the priest said people must do their best to keep their homes and themselves clean. In the stuffy church, Marie-Claire's head throbbed. The priest urged everyone to try to keep smallpox victims away from others in the family. But how could people do that? In small houses especially, and when many families in the city were sharing living space.

Oh, how hot the church was today. Hotter even than usual, and yet it hadn't been that hot outside, had it? Marie-Claire held her aching head between her hands as the priest droned on about the bishop advising people to stay home—even from church—if anyone in the family had smallpox.

The congregation listened in shocked silence.

"And it is imperative," the priest continued, "that you follow the advice of your medical doctors, even if they are recommending vaccination. Whatever steps can be taken to preserve the health of the body God has provided," he said, "must be taken."

Marie-Claire felt faint. What had happened to trusting in God? If God had sent smallpox because he was angry, would people staying away from church not make him angrier still? And yet, if you could catch smallpox from someone near you . . . Oh, with such a headache it was all just too confusing to think about. She leaned against Louis's shoulder and longed to go outside.

Finally, the service ended. It was cooler outside, but still Marie-Claire felt as if she was burning up, and so very tired. As big as she was, her brother picked her up and carried her all the way home.

That night she felt suddenly very cold, and sick to her stomach. Emilie wanted no blankets at all as Marie-Claire huddled beneath two. With her head still aching and a pain now stabbing her in the back, it took a long time to fall asleep. When finally she did, she dreamed terrible, vivid dreams.

Into the dark she called out, "Maman!"

Maman appeared by the side of her bed with a candle. "What is it, *chérie?*"

"Someone was chasing me, I do not know who. I ran and I ran but they were faster—"

"There, there. No one is chasing you. Put your head down on your pillow."

"Do you think we should have got the needle, Maman? I am frightened. I feel sick."

Maman stroked the damp wisps of Marie-Claire's hair from the side of her face. "Hush, go to sleep now, you will make yourself sicker with worry. I'm here, it's all right. You go to sleep." Maman stayed by Marie-Claire's side until she slept.

In the morning, her fever was gone. Her head and stomach felt fine.

"See what an overactive imagination can do?" Maman said.

But the next morning Marie-Claire was barely awake when Emilie yelled, "Oh, no!"

Marie-Claire knew without asking what was wrong, but part of her refused to believe it, even as she ran to the kitchen, fetched Papa's shaving mirror, and, afraid to look, held it against her chest.

She took a deep breath and whispered, "Please, God."

She looked in the mirror. Flat red spots covered her entire face.

Immediately she burst into tears.

When she pulled off her nightie, she saw her arms were spotted, too, and all across her chest.

"Marie-Claire," Emilie whined, "I don't feel well."

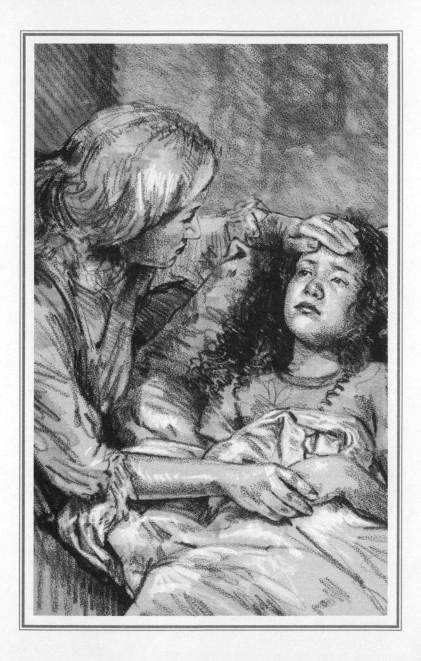

When Lucille and Bernadette came to the door, Maman said, "The girls cannot go with you to school. It has come here, *la picotte*."

"Oh, my, Tante Hélène, I am so sorry."

Soon Marie-Claire's spots rose on her face like pimples. Then they blistered. The lotion Maman stroked over her skin cooled the fiery rash, but only for a few minutes at a time.

At night Marie-Claire tossed and turned in her sleep. In the daytime she could no longer stand to look in the mirror at the mass of pus-oozing spots that marked her puffy face, and now Emilie's, too. "Please, God," she prayed, "do not let the horrid spots leave us with scars."

Maman interrupted her sewing to mop a cool wet cloth over the foreheads and necks of her daughters. Outside, something started banging against the house. Maman stomped downstairs, shouting, "As if we have not enough trouble here!"

When she came back upstairs, she shook in her hand a black-and-yellow notice. "SMALLPOX /

LA PICOTTE," it said. Maman crumpled the placard and stuffed it into the wood stove.

"Why is Maman so cross?" Emilie whispered.

"I hear you whispering," Maman said, "and I will tell you why I am cross. If the wrong people find out we have smallpox here, Papa and Louis will have to stay home from work, and Monsieur Grenier will bring me no more shirts to sew. How long do you think the food in our pantry will last if no one is earning, eh?"

Emilie began to cry. Aching and hot and too dull to offer comfort, Marie-Claire rolled over to face the wall. Her skin was on fire. She did not care if she lived or died.

The next day, the black wagon came.

CHAPTER N.º 6

"Please! No!" Maman begged.

But the men insisted, "You cannot keep the girls isolated here. Those sick with the pox must go to hospital if we are to contain it." They gathered Marie-Claire and Emilie in blankets, took them outside, and lifted them into the black wagon.

Huddled in the back, Marie-Claire closed her eyes. Terrified, she tried to pretend that the rough wagon was instead a fine carriage. It was not on its way to the smallpox hospital, but to a *soirée* at one of the mansions on the hill. The bumps she felt on her hands were not pox but beaded gloves. Instead of thin blankets, she and Emilie were wrapped in furs. And the horses clip-clopping in front of them were not mangy workhorses but glossy stallions.

"Are we going to die?" Emilie whined.

Marie-Claire answered, "Did Cendrillon die going to the ball?"

"Cendrillon?"

"Imagine, Emilie, that you are Cendrillon. You are on your way to a party finer than any you have ever seen. In which of these fine houses do you think your prince lives?" Marie-Claire straightened the blanket around Emilie's shoulders. "Mind your fur stole, *princesse*. Don't let it catch in the wheels of your fine carriage."

At the hospital, the putrid odour of smallpox filled the long room of beds. It was sweet and foul at the same time. From somewhere also came the stench of human waste. Marie-Claire covered her nose and mouth with her blanket, but it did not help.

"Where do we go to relieve ourselves?" she asked the nun who was showing them to their beds. Thankfully they were side by side.

The nun pointed to the end of the room.

The bucket of the commode was nearly full, but Marie-Claire had to use it.

Up and down both sides of the room, patients groaned and thrashed about in their beds. Nuns scurried from one bed to another with wet cloths, cups of water, and Bibles. Marie-Claire remembered what Lucille had said when she came out of hospital. *Can you imagine lying there and beside you in the next bed a girl has died? You call for the nuns to come, but* . . . Marie-Claire had been unable to imagine. Perhaps now she would not have to. So many patients. So few nuns— working as hard as they could, but always someone was in need.

"There's something nasty on my sheet," Emilie complained.

"I expect they haven't time to clean bedding between patients," Marie-Claire said. "Here, let's turn it over so you don't have to see that part."

"Can't we just share your bed?"

"I don't think so," Marie-Claire answered. "Not in a hospital."

But in the night Emilie crossed the small space between their beds to crawl in with Marie-Claire. In spite of how hot they felt, they held on to each other and tried to shut out the sounds of patients groaning and calling out, "Water! I need water!"

Once, after Emilie's breathing had grown regular, Marie-Claire heard a thump, as if someone had fallen out of bed. A moment later, she heard something being dragged across the floor. She looked up and realized what she had heard. It was not someone falling out of bed. A patient had died and been rolled off the bed in her sheet. Now her body was being taken to wherever bodies went before the cemetery.

Marie-Claire held her sleeping sister close. "Dear God, I do fear the ugly spots staying forever, but of me or Emilie dying I now have even more fear. I know you have many people to care for, but please remember, you have taken from our family already, through other sickness, my two baby brothers, Pierre and Philippe. To lose my little sister, too . . ." Marie-Claire let her tears flow over her bumpy face. God was taking so many lately. If he had a reason, what was it?

CHAPTER N.º 7

"Water! Please! I need water!"

For so long the woman had been calling. Why didn't she just go to sleep?

Because, Marie-Claire told herself, she is thirsty and too sick to get up for a drink. And perhaps she is also too afraid of dying to sleep.

Marie-Claire slipped from her bed and padded across the wood floor. "Where is your cup?" she asked. "I will get you some water."

Marie-Claire dipped the tin cup in the bucket of water by the door and returned to the woman's bedside. The woman drank. "God bless you, child. May you get your reward in heaven."

Marie-Claire returned to her bed, thinking she would prefer getting well and staying on earth to any reward that heaven might hold.

Soon her spots began to dry, but still Marie-Claire slept badly. All her fears for herself—and for Emilie, who slept so much—grew so large in her mind at night that there was no room, it seemed, for sleep. But she prayed, let her tears fall, and eventually sleep did come.

One morning, very early, before the nuns were about, one of the other patients came and stood by Marie-Claire's bed, her hands in the deep bulging pockets of her robe.

"We have been to the orchard," the woman said, "just a few of us. It is so lovely, with the moon going down on one side and the sun coming up on the other. Would you and your sister like an apple?" She held out two apples, red and shining.

"*Merci*," Marie-Claire said. "*Merci beaucoup.*"

Would she ever again get outside to look up at the moon and the sun? She was starting to feel better. For one thing, the spots no longer felt like little fires on her skin. Did that mean she was getting well?

Marie-Claire sank her teeth into her apple. Such a long time, it seemed, since she'd had one. Maman would surely bring apples if she were allowed to come, but since Lucille's time in hospital the rules had changed: no visitors except the priest. The apple was sweet, as if nipped by frost, but was it not still only September?

Juice dribbled down the skin of the apple as Marie-Claire took a second bite. She licked it off so as not to waste a single drop. She crunched again into the crisp fruit and prayed this would not be the last apple she would ever eat.

"*Viens*, Emilie. *Mange ta pomme.*"

"I can't." Emilie lay back on her pillow. "My

throat hurts." She let her apple, from which she had taken only a tiny bite, fall from her hand to the blanket.

"But you must eat," Marie-Claire insisted. "You must!"

The day Maman came to take her two daughters home, Sister Bernice met her at the door of the hospital with only one. The cry that rose from Maman—it was like someone had wrenched it, like a physical thing, from deep inside her. And then she was quiet.

Sister Bernice led Maman and Marie-Claire to the hospital chapel, where they stayed on their knees for a long time. But with Emilie gone, Marie-Claire thought, what was there to pray for—except perhaps an answer to why? Why did

Emilie have to die? Why did Emilie die and not me?

When Maman and Marie-Claire got home, Louis took Marie-Claire onto his lap. "It is a sad, sad thing," he said, "but I thank dear God that you were spared. Should you not do the same?"

"I try so hard to be good," Marie-Claire told him through her tears, "but God does not take only bad people. And do you know what, Louis? Maybe I do not even want any more to be alive."

"You must not say such a thing," Maman said. And then she did something Marie-Claire had never seen her do before. In the middle of the day, she went back to bed.

When Maman did not get up the next day, Marie-Claire stayed home from school to do the chores. It didn't matter, missing school. With her sister gone, she did not feel like going anyway.

All around the house Marie-Claire encountered

reminders of Emilie: her dress hanging on the hook by their bed, the chair where she sat at the table by the wood stove, the clothespin doll in the little dress Marie-Claire had sewn for her.

But Emilie herself was with the angels now. She had always liked stories about angels best, Marie-Claire remembered.

Maman rallied for the funeral mass and accepted the condolences of friends and relations, but when it was over, she sank again into her bed.

At supper one day Papa did his best to get Marie-Claire and Louis to talk about their activities.

"Today I swept the floor," Marie-Claire said. "I made the soup."

Louis said, "And very good soup it is, Marie-Claire." He sipped another mouthful from his spoon.

"And Louis, how was your day?"

Louis dropped his head and took a breath before looking up again and speaking. "Do you truly wish to hear how many houses I placarded? How many people I delivered to the hospital? How many chil—" His voice caught in his throat.

"I am sorry, *mon fils*. Of course we do not want to talk of such things."

The only sounds in the house then were the clinking of spoons against earthenware bowls, the snap of wood in the stove, and the snuffle of Papa blowing his nose into his handkerchief.

Marie-Claire was filling the dishpan with warm water from the stove when she stopped and looked at her brother. "Louis," she said, "how is it that you attend each day to people with smallpox and yet you do not get it yourself?"

"Perhaps it is the vaccination."

"Vaccination? You . . . ?" Marie-Claire glanced towards the door of the room where Maman lay awake in her bed.

"*Oui*. All the sanitary policemen have now been vaccinated. It is compulsory for us."

That night in bed, Marie-Claire heard Maman say to Papa, "Did I make a mistake, Josèph?

Should I have let that doctor who came here give the needle to the girls? Would Emilie . . . ?"

Marie-Claire could not bear the sound of her mother crying. She wanted to bury her head beneath her pillow, but she needed to hear Papa assuring Maman that no, of course she had done the right thing.

"I do not know, Hélène. I do not know."

He did not know? Even Papa was without answers to the awful questions raised, like ugly spots, by *la picotte*? How then would she, a mere ten-year-old girl, ever know anything?

Quietly, Maman said, "I do my best to take comfort in knowing that Emilie's soul is safe with God, as are those of dear little Pierre and Philippe, God bless them. But, oh, Josèph, I do miss all of my babies so."

"I know, *ma chérie*. I know."

To the sound of her parents strained voices saying the rosary, Marie-Claire did not fall asleep.

And Maman, again the next day, and the next, did not get out of bed.

CHAPTER N.º 9

At the market Marie-Claire trudged from stall to stall. She did not care if the cheese she bought was mouldy or the bread stale. As if it was not bad enough that she had lost a baby brother in the spring and now her little sister—oh, how she missed them both—now it seemed Maman was lost to her, too. Each morning she prayed that Maman would be her old self again, energetically pumping the treadle of the sewing machine.

But again Papa and Louis went off to work with the lunches Marie-Claire had made them.

And it was up to her also to clean the house, fetch water, do the marketing, and prepare meals. There was no time, again, for school or playing with Lucille. If Maman did not get up and start sewing soon, would they again have to take in boarders? Maybe that would not be such a bad thing. Having Maman in bed all day was so very lonely. With Tante Thérèse and Oncle Henri having moved to Toronto, it would have to be strangers this time.

Marie-Claire managed one day to get Maman to take a little soup, but only a little.

"Give her time, Marie-Claire," Papa said when he came home from work. "And remember her in your prayers."

How much time? Marie-Claire wondered. And how could Papa think she had not been praying for Maman? Her bad cough had almost disappeared, but what was wrong with her now was much more frightening. Could a person die of sadness? Why was God being so cruel to the Laroche family?

"Papa, I understand, of course, how very sad Maman must be. I am too. . ." Marie-Claire kept her eyes on the carrot she was chopping. "But should she not be getting back to sewing shirts for Monsieur Grenier?"

Papa sat down at the table where Marie-Claire was preparing vegetables. "Maman no longer has shirts to sew. Like many manufacturers in Montreal, Monsieur Grenier has lost many orders this month. He no longer needs your maman to work for him. But do not worry, Marie-Claire. With me working full time again, and your brother, we will not go hungry."

"Why did Monsieur Grenier lose orders? Men still need shirts, don't they?"

"Many English newspapers have overstated how badly *la picotte* is spreading. As a result, customers outside of Montreal do not want to buy goods that are made here—shirts, cigars—for fear they will get smallpox in their cities, too."

As Marie-Claire stirred the potatoes and carrots in the pot, the door banged open and

Louis's boisterous presence filled the room.

"Today I am a lucky man," he said.

"How so?" asked Papa.

"I went to a house on Rue Papineau to take *un enfant* to the hospital, and the mother came after me with an axe!"

"That does not sound very lucky to me," Marie-Claire cried.

"I am lucky," Louis said, "because I got away!"

In spite of her worry about Maman, Marie-Claire smiled.

"Five times five?" Louis snapped.

"Twenty-five."

"Seven times seven?"

"Louis, I am so glad you are home."

"Never mind your stalling. What is seven times seven?"

"I know it . . . forty-nine!"

Marie-Claire placed bowls of soup in front of Louis and Papa and joined them at the table with her own. Papa set aside the newspaper. "Another sad day coming," he said. "October sixteenth."

Marie-Claire sighed. Would not every day be sad, with their three little ones now dead and Maman almost as absent? Thank God Louis was home from the West, and for dear Papa.

"Ah yes," Louis said. He raised a spoonful of soup to his mouth. "The date they have set for the execution. Remember that man we heard speak? The one who said that instead of Riel it is the prime minister they should be hanging?"

Marie-Claire dipped a piece of bread in her soup. "I heard someone say today that Louis Riel is a madman."

"Riel is a great man," Papa said. "Just a little confused sometimes."

Marie-Claire, her own head so full of confusions these days, wanted to ask Papa what this great man was confused about, but the idea of grown men as confused as she was too troubling.

Papa changed the subject. "There is talk that the Health Department wants to make vaccination compulsory. Everyone will have to take the needle, whether they want to or not."

Louis said, "Some say it is the only way of stopping the spread of *la picotte*. Every week more people are dying than the week before."

"Still . . ." Papa licked soup from the corner of his moustache. "People should be allowed to decide such things for themselves."

"Papa," Marie-Claire said, "would it be a good idea for Maman to get a vaccination?"

"Why, *ma petite?*"

Marie-Claire wasn't sure. Something to do with needles and not being sick. But like everything else in her head, it was too confusing a thought to try to explain. And the needle wasn't for what was wrong with Maman anyway.

But there had to be something that could get Maman out of bed and wanting again to be alive. There just had to be.

An ice castle glistened in the centre of the city. Inside it Maman was queen and Papa king. Princesses Marie-Claire and Emilie rocked cradles in which babies slept contentedly. Maman laughed as Louis told stories, and servants rushed here and there bringing roast ham and fancy cake on fine crystal plates.

The plate holding the cake fell to the ice floor and smashed. And then another plate. And another. And Marie-Claire began to wake up. Far off, in the next street or perhaps the next, glass was breaking. Real glass. Someone shouted, "Down with compulsory vaccination!"

Other voices shouted, "Clear the streets! Go on home!"

More glass breaking.

"Bravo Louis Riel!"

"Down with compulsory vaccination!"

"*Vive la France!*"

A candle approached Marie-Claire across the dark room.

"Maman?"

"Maman is sleeping." Papa sat on the edge of the bed. "The sounds outside woke me. I was concerned that if you were awake you might be frightened."

"What is happening, Papa?"

"Some people, angry about the vaccination, are creating a disturbance."

"But, Papa . . ." Again Marie-Claire's thoughts were too confused to express.

"Yes?" Papa stroked Marie-Claire's head. "Take your time, *chérie.*"

"Is it possible that the vaccination is a good thing? Maybe it gives some people smallpox but keeps other people from getting it. I keep thinking that maybe if . . ." Marie-Claire squeezed her eyes shut. She could not bring herself to say it.

"I know what you keep thinking. They are the same thoughts your maman keeps having, and it is making it hard for her to get out of bed."

Outside, the sounds of shouting and breaking glass grew quieter. "The men must be moving farther away," Marie-Claire said.

"Your maman will get up one day soon," Papa said. "You will see."

Marie-Claire nodded, wanting to believe him. "Go back to bed, Papa. You must be getting chilly in your nightshirt. Thank you, Papa, for coming to talk to me."

Before returning to his bed, Papa hugged Marie-Claire close and rocked her like a baby.

CHAPTER N.º 11

From the pulpit, the priest said, "As the church ministers to men's souls, doctors minister to men's bodies. Their vaccination may well be part of curing our city of the smallpox which has smitten us. The bishop himself has been re-vaccinated this week as an example to all of God's children. But as important as ever in fighting this battle are repentance, humility, and prayer. Let us pray."

On her knees between Papa and Louis, Marie-Claire prayed. She prayed for an end to the smallpox. But, even more, she prayed that Maman's spirit would somehow be restored.

"We shall hold a procession this week marking the annual Feast of the Rosary. We will implore the Virgin Mary to intercede with God to stay the smallpox epidemic. If you have smallpox in your family, however, we do urge you to stay away. Just as, if you have smallpox in your family, you should not be here today."

Smallpox, smallpox. Did the priest forget that people had other troubles besides smallpox? And if more had been said sooner about vaccinating and staying away, might Emilie's life have been spared, and what was now happening to Maman avoided?

Outside the church, after mass, the priest stood on the top step, shaking hands with his parishioners as they left. Some stopped to chat for a moment. Could she, Marie-Claire, talk to the priest, instead of just timidly shaking his hand as she usually did? She was a little frightened of him, with his long robes and spiky eyebrows. But his voice was always so strong and sure. Could he, somehow, help her feel more strong and sure? About . . . anything?

As Marie-Claire, Louis, and Papa neared the door, she said, "Wait. I may have left something behind." Louis and Papa stepped out of line to let others go ahead while Marie-Claire made her way back into the church and to the pew where they had been sitting.

She crouched down pretending to look for something. It was a silly thing to have said. She had brought nothing with her to church that she might have left behind. But when she rejoined Papa and Louis, they were, as she had hoped they would be, last in the line of people waiting to shake hands with the priest.

When his large hands encircled hers, Marie-Claire made herself say, "Please, Father, may I speak with you for a moment?"

Papa looked surprised.

"Certainly, my child," the priest said, "come back inside."

"We'll wait for you here," Louis said.

"No, you and Papa go ahead," Marie-Claire said bravely. "I can get home on my own, and

Maman is there alone." She watched them walk down the steps to the road.

The priest said, "I hope that your maman does not now have smallpox?"

"No, Father, she has a sickness . . . of the heart."

Sitting with the priest in a pew near the front of the church, with candles burning nearby and the smell of incense hanging in the air, Marie-Claire took a deep breath. Then she described Maman's inability to get out of bed, her lack of appetite. "And sometimes," she said, "I hear her weeping in the night. I have prayed for her, Father, and do all I can to help at home . . ." Marie-Claire felt tears pushing themselves from her eyes.

"You are a fine girl, Marie-Claire, in a fine family. A family that has suffered greatly through this year. I will add to those prayers you are saying for your mother a special one of my own. Do you know, is your mother herself praying at this difficult time?"

"She still says the rosary with Papa at bedtime."

"That is a hopeful sign. Perhaps if I were to pay

your maman a visit . . ."

"Father . . ." Marie-Claire hesitated to go on. "There is . . . something else."

"Something else?"

"When the men came to give me and Emilie the needle . . . Maman sent them away." Marie-Claire hung her head, feeling Maman's shame as she spoke. "But" —Tears caught in her throat— "it was not her fault, Father.—She thought . . . My Tante Thérèse said—"

"Of course it was not her fault." The priest took Marie-Claire's hand in his. "If even the doctors, whose domain it is to know the ways of the body, could not agree whether vaccination was a good thing or bad, how could your maman know? How could any of us? Your maman must not blame herself for smallpox coming to your family, but do her best to trust again in God." The priest stood. "I will visit her soon."

"Thank you, Father."

After the priest left, Marie-Claire stayed seated in her pew a little longer, trying to let his assurances and the peacefulness of the empty church calm her.

How could any of us? he had said. Did that mean even men of the Church were sometimes confused about what was right? She wasn't sure if that made her feel better about her own confusion, or worse.

On her way out, Marie-Claire stopped at the back of the church. By the bank of candles, she pushed a coin through the slot in the donation box, heard its satisfying clink as it landed among other coins, and took a taper from the holder. She held it to the flame of an already-lit candle, then lit a candle of her own.

"Please, God, help Maman to get back her trust in you, and also her spirit for living. And please, if you can, help me be not so confused all the time?"

Her candle strongly aflame, Marie-Claire plunged the burning end of the taper that she had used to light it into the receptacle of ashes.

"Amen."

CHAPTER Nº 12

It was a gorgeous fall day—cool, crisp, and sunny. A churchman in flaming red robes led thousands of people through the streets, chanting, praying, and saying their rosaries. Twelve men carried a brass statue of the Virgin Mary that, it was said, had helped ward off cholera when that disease had come to the city some years before. Surely, people were saying, it could do the same for the smallpox. And if the doctors, too, were doing what they felt was necessary. . . .

Marie-Claire wasn't sure.

In the days following the procession, the streets were quiet places. They still reeked of disinfectant. Black wagons continued to deliver sick people to hospital. The blinds on many houses were down. Few children played outside. But Marie-Claire wondered, did any of it matter? In spite of the visit from the priest, Maman remained in bed, and Marie-Claire felt no closer to having answers to her many questions, the most pressing one being: how to get Maman up.

If Jesus were here, he would probably lay his hands on Maman's head or feet and she would miraculously rise from her bed. Marie-Claire tried this once herself. Maman said, "You are a sweet child, Marie-Claire." But she did not get up.

After supper one night Louis gave a gloomy report. "Every month the number of smallpox deaths has tripled. There have been almost fifteen hundred this month alone," he said, "and that does not include the nearby villages where there have been many deaths also."

Marie-Claire could not begin to imagine, as

she washed the dishes by lamplight, what fifteen hundred people would look like, but it had to be quite a crowd. She pictured row upon row of church pews full of people. Would each pew hold ten people? Fifteen rows would be . . . only one hundred and fifty. Both sides of the church . . . three hundred. That many again, and again, and again, and again? That's how many had died, just from smallpox, in one month?!

Why, that must mean that most of the people at the market, in shops, and in the streets knew someone who had died. So many sad people in one city. Was Maman the only one so grief-stricken to take to her bed and stay there? Perhaps not.

Whether she was or not didn't matter. Tomorrow, Marie-Claire decided as she dumped the dishwater in the laneway, when Papa and Louis were gone to work, she would get Maman out of bed.

The bells of all the churches began suddenly to toll. It was the first of November, the Month of the Dead. Every night at eight o'clock, throughout the month, the bells would toll. A call to prayer for the souls of those who had died.

In the cool night air, Marie-Claire paused to bow her head.

The next morning she woke early and emptied the chamber pots in the back-lane privy before anyone else was up. She lit the fire in the wood stove and fried some bread for breakfast. She handed Papa and Louis their lunch boxes. When they had left for work, Marie-Claire marched into Maman's room.

Maman lay curled up on her side facing the wall. The covers were pulled up high around her ears. Her hair was splayed in greasy strings across her pillow. The air in the room was stale.

Marie-Claire flung open the window. The breeze that blew in was raw. Before she lost her nerve, Marie-Claire took hold of a lump that might be Maman's arm, shook it, and said, "Time to get up."

"Soon," Maman muttered, rolling back over. "I will get up soon."

"Soon is not soon enough." Marie-Claire again forced her maman to face the room. "It is weeks now since Emilie died. You must get out of bed."

Maman closed her eyes and groaned.

"Don't!" Marie-Claire shouted. "In case you have not noticed, you have another daughter. Me! And you are not the only one who feels badly that Emilie is gone! Do you not care that I have lost my sister? That alone every day I do all the chores for this family because you choose to stay in your bed? For all the use you are to anyone around here, you might as well—"

Marie-Claire stopped. She did not mean that. She took a deep breath to calm herself.

"Maman," Marie-Claire said again, "you must get up. Perhaps if you come to church just once, if you say there a special prayer for Emilie . . . ?"

It was no use. Maman had again rolled over. She was sobbing, it seemed, into her pillow. Her arms were up around her head.

Marie-Claire shouted, "You do not care about me at all, do you?! Instead of Emilie, perhaps I should have been the one to die!" Marie-Claire ran from Maman's bedside and out of the house, with no idea at all where she was going.

She had not gone far when she smelled smoke and heard the clanging of bells.

Fire!

CHAPTER N° 13

On the next street, from windows upstairs and down, flames licked and black smoke billowed. Whose house was burning? No one seemed to know. Firemen were jumping down from wagons. Was Papa here somewhere? Had he even had time yet this morning to get to the fire station?

Marie-Claire spotted him at the door of the house, barring a woman from entering.

"But my baby," the woman wailed, "he is inside."

"Please stand back," Papa said. "We will do our best to get him out. Is there anyone else inside?"

"No. But please, my baby . . ." The woman scurried over to a pair of children huddled by the hose wagon. "*Mes enfants*, you must—" But she did not finish her sentence. Among all the clamouring and shouting and the snapping of flames, she ran back to the house. Again a fireman prevented her from entering. Papa had gone inside.

Marie-Claire fought the urge to join the woman at the door, to push her way into the burning house and make her papa come out. Flames were darting now along another window frame. Could a baby possibly still be alive in there?

A fireman pointed a hose at the spreading flames of the burning house. Another was hosing down the house beside it. Marie-Claire remembered Papa saying that if one house on these streets caught fire, others were likely to catch, too. So close together, and made of wood . . .

The crowd grew. Along the street trotted more horses pulling more fire wagons and snorting in the smoky air.

Oh, why did Papa have to be the fireman to go inside? Why could he not stand outside with a hose?

Beside Marie-Claire, the young children whose house was burning began to cry. Someone tried to interest them in feeding the horses lumps of sugar, but it did no good.

Marie-Claire ran to the woman at the door, crying for her baby inside. She knew it was cruel but she shouted, "Madame, there is nothing you can do for your baby! You have two other children who need you! I will wait here, and if someone brings your baby out, I will come right away and tell you! But you must go—now—and be with your other children!"

As if all the young mother had truly needed was someone to tell her what to do, she staggered to the hose wagon and gathered her two youngsters in her arms. From inside the house came a loud crash.

Whoosh! Flames shot up a wall where a moment before there had been none. A fireman high on a ladder, hosing down the upstairs of the house, aimed instead in the direction of the new flames. Pushing Marie-Claire and the crowd into the street, another fireman shouted, "Stand back!"

As Marie-Claire stumbled backwards, a figure huddled around a bundle staggered out of the burning house. With his blackened face, it took Marie-Claire a moment to recognize him.

"Papa!" She skirted past everyone and ran to him. "Papa, are you all right?!"

He coughed and coughed and handed her the bundle wrapped in a blanket. The bundle wiggled.

It was the baby! She was holding the baby, and the baby was alive!

"Oh, Papa!" Marie-Claire cried.

Just then a fireman shouted, "Josèph! Over here!" and Papa ran to help beat back flames breaking through yet another wall. It was going to take some time to get a fire this bad under control.

But the baby was safe. Thanks to Papa, the baby was safe!

Marie-Claire ran to the woman with the children. All three of them were sitting with their backs to the destruction of their home. Above the crackling and the hissing of the fire and the chatter of the gathering crowd, Marie-Claire heard them singing. "*Quel ami fidèle et tendre, Nous avons en Jésus Christ. Toujours prêt à nous entendre, A répondre à notre cri* . . ."

"Madame?" Marie-Claire said.

When the woman looked up, Marie-Claire crouched down and handed her the baby. With the children, she continued to sing where their mother had left off. "*Il connaît nos défaillances, Nos chutes de chaque jour. Sévère en ses exigences, Il est riche en son amour.*"

From down the street came snorting horses pulling more fire wagons. And more.

"Madame," Marie-Claire said, "will you come with me? You and your children? I live close by and you can stay at my house until . . ."

Until when? Even when the firemen were successful in putting out the fire, this family would have no home to return to. Was she inviting them to stay until they found another place to live? With Maman still confined to her bed, and this a family with two children and a baby?

But what else could she do?

CHAPTER N.º 14

As their footsteps clanged up the stairs, Marie-Claire tried to explain, "My maman is not well, but do not worry. She does not have the smallpox."

"Perhaps it would be better—" the woman behind her began to say.

But meeting Marie-Claire at the door was Maman.

"*Mon Dieu*, Marie-Claire, thank God you are home. I wanted to come and find you but I had no idea where to begin looking. What you said, *ma fille*, it was true, but not that I do not care. I—" Maman stopped, suddenly noticing the people on the stairs behind her daughter.

"Their house is burning, Maman. Papa saved the baby."

"I should have realized when I saw the smoke where you would be. Papa . . . ?"

"Papa is fine. He and many firemen are still fighting the fire, but they will not be able to save the house."

"And so . . ."—Maman's voice was deep—"you invited them to stay here?"

Had the invitation been a mistake? These frightened people had lost so much. It had felt so right.

"I did, Maman," said Marie-Claire.

It still felt so very clearly like the only thing she could have done. Just as yelling at Maman had earlier, even if Maman did not— But Maman *did* get up. She *was* up. She was dressed and she had combed her hair.

Maman folded Marie-Claire in her arms. "Oh,

my brave daughter! I am so proud of you!" To the strangers on the steps, she said, "Come in. Please. You must stay as long as you need to."

On the table was a sack of flour and some eggs.

Marie-Claire touched her mother's sleeve and whispered, "I am proud of you, too, Maman."

Maman put the kettle on for tea. Before joining the mothers at the table, Marie-Claire found Emilie's clothespin doll and puzzle for the children to play with. And at last everyone introduced themselves.

"Did you say," Madame Linteau asked Marie-Claire, "that the fireman who saved Michel's life is your papa?"

"Yes," Marie-Claire said, bouncing the baby on her knee, "I did."

"Madame Laroche," Madame Linteau said, "what a fine family you have!"

"I do," Maman said. "I most certainly do."

The Linteaus were still staying with Marie-Claire's family mid-November when Papa came home holding a newspaper limply in one hand. "They have done it," he said. "Louis Riel has been hanged."

Monsieur Linteau groaned. Louis cursed, "*C'est une abomination!*"

Marie-Claire set the last spoon at its place on the table. "Was that not supposed to happen some time ago, Papa?"

"It should never have happened. Riel's execution is an attack on all French people in Canada." Papa shook his head. "But you are right. His execution has been scheduled and rescheduled several times now."

Over City Hall, the flag of France flew at half-mast. A special mass was planned in Riel's honour. Monsieur Linteau, Papa, and Louis went off together to the Champs-de-Mars to hear famous men speak of the great man who was now dead. When they returned home, they agreed around the table that a grave injustice had been done.

Marie-Claire had noticed in the newspapers Papa brought home that many words had been written about this one man, but not one about all the people still dying of smallpox. Where, she wondered, was the justice in that?

CHAPTER N°15

On the last day of November, Marie-Claire was feeding Michel his bottle, Madame Linteau was stirring a pot of stew on the wood stove, Papa was playing a quiet tune on his harmonica, and Maman was slicing a loaf of bread into thick pieces. She was doing so much better now. She got out of bed every day, and only occasionally did Marie-Claire catch her staring at nothing.

In the corner, the two Linteau children began to laugh. Monsieur Linteau was showing them how he could remove his thumb and stick it back on.

How dear Emilie would have loved such a trick. Marie-Claire sighed. How Emilie would have loved such a full and busy house.

Marie-Claire lowered Michel into the cradle as the nightly bells tolled for the last time. Against her back blew a sudden gust of icy air.

Louis banged shut the door, hung his coat on a peg, and breathlessly announced, "The smallpox news is good. Half the number of deaths this month as last. *La picotte* at last is being driven out of the city!" He grabbed Marie-Claire and lifted her high in the air.

"That is good," Papa said. "Very good."

"*Encore*," insisted one of the Linteau children. "Do it again."

Monsieur Linteau again took hold of his thumb.

"I have news today, too," Maman said. She pulled a letter from the pocket of her apron. "Tante Thérèse and Oncle Henri are now parents of a baby girl. Her name is Angelique. They plan to come visit as soon as Thérèse feels strong enough to travel."

Angelique. It was a beautiful name.

"We may have a very crowded house again," Papa said, "if the Linteaus are still with us then."

"Yes!" Marie-Claire beamed, hugging Louis tight around the neck. "And won't a crowded house be wonderful?"

"Indeed it will," agreed Maman. "Indeed it will."

Against the window of the Laroche home, fresh big flakes of snow began to fall.

BOOK THREE

Visitors

CHAPTER N° 1

Marie-Claire felt a tugging on her skirt as she cut lard into the flour.

"Can't you *please* leave me alone?"

She was tired of André's constant demands for attention. She was tired of the whole Linteau family. Madame Linteau's shrill voice grated on her nerves. The oily smell of the factory clung to Monsieur Linteau's clothing when he came in from work, and his sweat didn't have the pleasant earthiness of Papa's. The Linteau children's endless tugging on her skirts made it almost impossible to get chores done. And the baby . . . well, he couldn't help it if his skin was sore from where his wet diapers rubbed, and who wouldn't cry with pain like that? Still, Marie-Claire couldn't help feeling sorry she had ever invited the Linteaus to stay that day their house burned down. Why couldn't they just hurry up and find a new home?

Such selfish thoughts. Marie-Claire scolded herself for them immediately. She left the pastry she was making for the next day's fish pie and wiped her hands on her apron so she could help little André with the string game he had managed to get tangled up in knots.

"Marie-Claire," Maman said, helping Madame Linteau with the washing and drying of supper dishes, "when you have finished there, will you please put on some more water? Madame Linteau would like the children to have a bath tonight before bed."

Another bath meant filling the *big* kettle. Had Priscille and André not bathed last week? Surely they did not need to wash again already! But Marie-Claire knew better than to argue. She handed André back his untangled string. "What do you say?"

"Not like that," André whined. "You were supposed to keep the end tied up."

Marie-Claire snapped, "The answer I was looking for was *Merci!*" Keep the end tied up? Why did nothing this little boy said ever make sense? With her little sister, Emilie, there had always been instant understanding, even at times when Emilie had trouble finding the right words.

Marie-Claire emptied what was left of the water in the bucket into the big kettle on the stove and took the bucket to the door. As she wrapped her shawl around her shoulders, Papa said, "Let me do that, Marie-Claire."

"I'll help too," Monsieur Linteau said, fetching another bucket from behind the curtain, where such things were stored.

"Thank you." Marie-Claire went back to her pastry while the men went to fill the buckets from the tap in the back lane and Maman and Madame Linteau finished putting away the supper dishes.

When Madame Linteau began to stoke the fire in the wood stove, Priscille tugged her skirt. "Let me put a stick in," she pleaded, "let me!"

Marie-Claire wanted to scold Priscille for speaking so rudely. Emilie, who had been no older than Priscille, would never have spoken to Maman like that. Maman would never have stood for it. But once when the Linteaus were out, Marie-Claire had commented to Maman about Priscille and André's poor manners, and she had just said that different families had different ways of doing things, they mustn't judge, and Marie-Claire most certainly must not say anything of the children's manners to Madame Linteau.

"Ow! Ow!" Priscille jumped up and down, waving her hand madly in the air.

"Oh, my darling." Madame Linteau rushed to console her daughter.

"You should never have let your *darling* . . ." Marie-Claire began.

With a sharp look, Maman stopped her from finishing. "Seeing as you are the oldest, Marie-

Claire, perhaps you would like to have the first bath tonight." Maman set the tin washtub on the floor by the stove and moved the privacy curtain into place.

As the water heated, Monsieur Linteau gathered his children—one under each arm—for a story. Madame Linteau discreetly settled Michel to her breast for a feeding. Papa and Louis played a game of cards, and Maman took up some mending. Marie-Claire wrapped her finished pastry in a cloth and set it on the windowsill. December was cold enough not to have to put it in the icebox, especially at night.

But beside the wood stove it was cozy-warm. Marie-Claire tested the water and emptied the heavy kettle into the tub. She got the bar of soap from the shelf in the pantry, and a washrag. She stripped out of her clothes and stepped quickly into the ankle-deep water.

Such a luxury to get the first bath, before the water cooled and grew scummy with soap. It was kind of Maman to suggest it, before Madame

Linteau got to it first with her *darling* André or Priscille. Just the same, Marie-Claire washed in a hurry, not trusting the Linteau children to leave her alone once their story was finished.

"I hear that the Saint-Jean Baptiste Society is planning a special mass at Notre Dame for the repose of Louis Riel's spirit," Papa said as he shuffled the deck of cards.

"We should go early," Louis said. "It is bound to attract quite a crowd."

Marie-Claire stepped from the tub. Another good thing about getting the first bath was that the towel was not yet damp, as it would be for those who followed. She heard Maman say, "Let's hope the crowds do not spread smallpox again, as it is said they did last spring."

"Not too much danger of that," Louis said. "Few new cases have been reported this week except at the insane asylum and in one of the outlying villages."

Drying herself off, Marie-Claire noticed smallpox marks on her arms that had not yet completely faded, in spite of it being almost three months since she and poor Emilie had had the horrid disease.

"Are you finished back there, Marie-Claire?" Maman asked.

"Yes. I was just about to get into my nightgown."

"Here." Maman passed her another around the privacy screen. "I mended your clean one today, if you would like to wear it instead."

"Thank you." Marie-Claire pulled the clean nightgown over her head. It smelled fresher than the one she'd been about to put on, but its sleeves barely covered her elbows. Squares of material— cut from an old nightgown of Emilie's, Marie-Claire could not help noticing—patched places that were so thin the fabric was starting to shred.

Back in the main room, Maman poked her darning needle into a heavy woollen sock. Madame Linteau placed her sleeping baby into the cradle and began to undress Priscille for her bath. Marie-Claire stared out the black window into the night. Why did she so resent the Linteau children, feel so irritated by almost everything they did? She stroked the Emilie-nightgown patches on her elbows. How was it, she wondered, that they had escaped getting small-pox when so many other children, including herself and Emilie, had not? Had André and Priscille perhaps been given the awful vaccina-tion that some doctors said could keep you well? Louis said people who hadn't yet had smallpox now *had* to get the needle, or else pay a fine.

At the far end of the room from the wood stove, Marie-Claire crawled under the blanket on her bed. But with Madame Linteau's shrill voice still filling the house, and Priscille and André soon crowding her for space, it would be some time before she would sleep. Realizing she had forgot-ten to say her prayers, Marie-Claire climbed out of bed again. The floor was cold on her knees.

"Please God, help the Linteaus to find a new home soon." Scrambling back under the blanket she added, "Tomorrow, please, if you are not too busy?"

CHAPTER N°2

In the back lane, Marie-Claire stamped her feet, trying to keep warm as she waited for Monsieur Linteau to finish his business in the outhouse. He was even slower in there than her downstairs neighbour, Monsieur Flaubert. She counted the puffs of her breath hanging in the cold air, trying to be patient. Too often last winter, Marie-Claire remembered, she had been scolded for pleading with Monsieur Flaubert to hurry up.

Down the metal stairs on the back of her house clattered André, and when the outhouse door opened, he hurtled past her.

"Wait your turn!" Marie-Claire shouted. "It's not fair!"

"I cannot wait." André grabbed himself urgently.

"Go then. Go." Marie-Claire had no interest in laundering the boy's pants.

After a breakfast of fried bread and beans, Marie-Claire hurried to meet Lucille. The muddy road was hard and bumpy beneath her feet. More than once, she almost turned her ankle in one of the many ruts. At the corner, her cousin was hopping impatiently from one foot to another.

"I am sorry I am late."

Lucille grabbed Marie-Claire by the arm and together they walked into the brisk wind. "Don't tell me. The Linteaus again, right?"

"Do you think I'm a terrible person to wish them gone?"

"I think you are funny."

"Funny?" Marie-Claire said indignantly.

"Was it not you who invited them to stay?"

"But for *six weeks* they have been with us! And still their old house is no more than a heap of ashes! I did not know it would be so long."

"Having them has not been all bad. It seems, for instance, that your Maman's new friendship with Madame Linteau is helping to keep her from slipping back into the awful doldrums of the fall, *n'est-ce pas?*"

Marie-Claire clutched her shawl, its end flapping in the wind, more firmly in her fist. "I suppose."

"And have you not told me a number of times about games that Monsieur Linteau plays with André and Priscille which make you laugh?"

Marie-Claire sighed. "True. For a while I loved cuddling little Michel, too. But now—"

"Never mind. At school you can forget about your problems at home. But hurry. We mustn't be late."

"If we are late"—Marie-Claire laughed— "then Sister Chantal's punishment will also help me forget!"

At the next corner a tinsmith was lighting his charcoal fire. Marie-Claire would have loved to stop and watch him mending things, but today there were no extra minutes to spare. She and Lucille hurried past.

"Where is your sister this morning?" Marie-Claire asked.

"When you were not yet at our meeting corner, I sent her ahead with a friend," Lucille said. "I knew she would have trouble keeping up with us."

Just then, from the next block, came the clanging of the handbell calling the girls into school. Marie-Claire and Lucille ran as fast as they could. They arrived out of breath just as the last girls were going through the doors. Sister Chantal looked down at them as they passed and shook her head.

Marie-Claire and Lucille took their seats on opposite sides of the room. They had been caught talking once too often when they were supposed to be memorizing their Bible verses, and Sister Chantal no longer allowed them to sit together.

Through the morning's opening prayers, Marie-Claire kept her head bowed. She listened attentively as Sister Chantal read to the girls from the Bible—until she noticed, in a seat nearby, that Jacqueline was back at school today. She was one of the last girls at school to have been kept home with smallpox.

Jacqueline turned to look out the window. The side of her face was still badly marked. The rhythm of Sister Chantal's voice told Marie-Claire that the reading was nearing its end. She forced her eyes back to the nun.

Before Sister Chantal could begin to ask the girls questions about what she had read, the head Sister came to the door and called Sister Chantal away. All the girls knew without being told that they should take up their samplers and quietly practise their stitching when their teacher was out of the room, but everyone was excited that Jacqueline was back at school, and slowly the chatter around her built.

"Did you suffer badly?"

"It was as if I were on fire. I thought I would die. And when the scabs began to fall off . . ."

Jacqueline shuddered. "It was too disgusting for words."

Marie-Claire knew from experience that what Jacqueline said was no exaggeration.

"Did you hear about poor Hilde?" someone said. "The pox went right into her eyes, and now she is blind."

When exclamations of sympathy and disgust had died down, another girl said to Jacqueline, "Did you try charcoal on your spots? My Tante Elaine says if you use it soon enough, a paste with charcoal in it will make all signs of the pox disappear."

Several girls began to argue about whether Jacqueline had any hope of getting rid of her old spots, or would be scarred for life. One girl said her mother still had scars from when she'd had smallpox as a girl, the last time the sickness had come to the city.

Marie-Claire heard footsteps outside the room. "Shh!" she said, and quickly bowed her head over her stitching.

Several girls were caught chattering and Sister Chantal made them stay after school. Marie-Claire knew they would be in for quite a scolding. Luckily both she and Lucille were free to go at the end of the day.

In spite of the cold, they walked at a leisurely pace, and even took a long way home so they could look at the shop windows all decked out for Christmas. Shivering against the wind, and blowing on her hands to keep them warm, Lucille said, "It feels as if it will snow soon."

Marie-Claire sniffed the cold air. "I hope it stays this time." The last snowfall had melted the day after it fell.

In and out of shops, finely dressed ladies bustled. Lucille nudged Marie-Claire's arm as one whose fur coat almost reached the ground walked by.

"It is a shame," the lady was saying to her friend, "that some mothers do not know how to properly dress their youngsters at this time of year."

"Very typical of *those* people," the other lady answered.

Marie-Claire knew enough English to understand what they were saying, but it took her a moment to realize that it was she and Lucille that the women were speaking of.

"What does she mean—*those people*?"

"She might mean people without much money," Lucille guessed. "Or—Maman says the English people are snobs, so she might mean people who are French."

"Well, la-de-da," said Marie-Claire. After checking that no one but Lucille could see her, she stuck her tongue out at the rich lady's back.

CHAPTER N°. 3

On Saturday there was no school to escape to, but mercifully, after breakfast, Madame Linteau announced that she was taking both children and the baby out—in search of a new home, and then to shop for clothes to wear to their uncle's wedding. The only clothing they had was what they'd been wearing when their house caught fire. Maman would do the marketing, she said, and headed out. The men, of course, were at work. Marie-Claire took up the straw broom and began to sweep.

How quiet the house was with everyone gone.

Not in the sad way it had been in the days imme-diately after Emilie's passing, when Maman was too weary and discouraged to get out of bed, but in a peaceful way that helped Marie-Claire settle her thoughts about all that had happened this year. Perhaps today the Linteaus would be successful in their search for a new home. Surely in this big city there was room for them somewhere. Three chil-dren did not make for such a very large family.

With the floors all swept, Marie-Claire leaned the broom in the corner. How tempting it was to crawl back into bed for a little more sleep while the house was quiet, but there was still work to be done. She couldn't leave it all for Maman. It had to be hard on her, too, having an extra family under foot all the time. And before long, her Tante Thérèse and Oncle Henri would be coming to stay with their new baby, Angélique. Unless there wasn't room! How awful it would be if they decided not to come from Toronto to visit because there was no room for them!

As if continuing to be helpful might encourage

God to answer her prayers for a new home for the Linteaus, Marie-Claire began to tidy the house. She hung Madame Linteau's nightgown on a hook. She gathered the pieces of a puzzle Priscille had left on the floor—Marie-Claire had lazily swept around it—into a tidy pile. She carried Papa's shaving mirror from the table to the windowsill.

Since seeing her marked face in Papa's mirror the morning she had woken with smallpox, Marie-Claire had avoided her reflection. But now, three months after coming home from the smallpox hospital, she held up the shaving mirror and forced herself to look.

Her many spots had faded greatly. Most had completely disappeared. But the marks of a few, especially where several of the flaming spots had been clumped together, were quite awful. Now that Marie-Claire was looking in the mirror, it was hard to stop looking. The longer she looked, the more spots she saw. The more spots she saw, the uglier she felt!

But hadn't someone at school yesterday said . . .

Marie-Claire threw a shawl around her shoulders, grabbed a tin cup, and went outside. She strode quickly to a place in the street where the remains of charcoal fires were often dumped, dug past the damp layer on top, and gathered some dry charcoal dust into the cup.

Back in the kitchen, she spooned a little cornstarch into the charcoal dust and dribbled in a handful of water from the bucket beside the wood stove. With a small spoon, she stirred until the mixture made a thin paste.

How cold it was on her finger, and smooth. Looking carefully into Papa's shaving mirror, Marie-Claire started dabbing the paste onto her face—on a spot up near her eyebrow, on the two spots on her forehead, and on one beside her nose. Oh, and there was another spot right in the middle of her cheek. Soon her face was dotted with blobs of dark grey mud.

It looked worse than it had before. But if what Micheline had said was true . . . ? Noticing another spot in the crease by her chin, Marie-Claire dipped her finger again into the muddy paste.

"Marie-Claire, what are you doing?"

"Louis! I thought you were out!" Behind the grey splotches, Marie-Claire felt her face redden. But thank goodness it was her brother who'd caught her and not Maman. Louis might think she looked ridiculous with mud on her face, but Maman would consider what she was up to sinful vanity, or, at the very least, conceited shenanigans. Either way, she'd have no patience with any of it.

"What are you doing to your face?" Louis asked.

"Trying to get rid of my spots. No one will ever want to marry such an ugly—"

"Marry! You are ten years old!"

"Almost eleven."

"And a beautiful almost-eleven you are, too." Louis held Marie-Claire by the shoulders, stared into her face, and grinned. "Except for that mud you have plastered all over yourself."

"Someone at school said charcoal could help get rid of smallpox spots."

Marie-Claire checked the mirror to see if she had missed any. With a damp washrag she dabbed away one of the first blobs of paste she had applied. Except for being a little grey now, the old spot looked the same as it had before.

"Maybe the mud has to be on longer," she said, "or maybe I have to put it on several times for it to work."

"Do you really think so?"

Marie-Claire sighed. "If I had lots of money," she said, "I could buy the special cream that gets rid of them."

"What cream is that?"

"It was in the newspaper. If you send your money to a man in Boston he will mail you a cream made in England guaranteed to remove smallpox marks. *Guaranteed!* But, Louis, for the amount it costs, it would be possible to buy five or six chickens!"

"Listen to me. A few little spots cannot keep you from being the beautiful person God made you. You have no need of charcoal or of any creams."

"No?"

"No. But Marie-Claire, you do need . . ." Louis's tone was very serious, ". . . to wash your face."

"You tease!" Marie-Claire flicked the damp washrag at her brother. He grabbed it away from her and dipped it in the bucket.

"Don't!" she yelled. "Don't!"

Louis grinned. Marie-Claire scooted behind the table to get away from him. He took a sudden step around the end of the table as if to come at her with the drippy cloth.

"Louis, no! I'll do it myself!"

Louis laughed and let her snatch the cloth.

Marie-Claire wiped the bits of charcoal paste from her face. The spots were still there, and they weren't pretty, no matter what her brother said. She had a feeling, deep down, that the paste was not going to work, no matter how long she left it or how many times she applied it.

To keep herself from crying, Marie-Claire tried changing the subject. "Why are you home so early? I thought you had to work today."

"With so few new cases of smallpox, there is little to do. I had just one SMALLPOX/LA PICOTTE notice to put up, and two trips to make with the black wagon. Is that not wonderful news for just before Christmas?"

Not wonderful enough to help me, Marie-Claire thought miserably.

Immediately she scolded herself for thinking so selfishly when her sister and many others had lost not just their prettiness to the dreadful small-pox, but their lives.

Dear Emilie. At the thought of Christmas coming without her, Marie-Claire's shoulders sagged.

"Why did *la picotte* come here, Louis? Will I ever stop missing Emilie so? Sometimes when I think of her, it is as if claws are raking across my heart."

Louis sat down by the table and took Marie-Claire into his lap. "Gradually, *ma chérie,* this wound in your heart will heal. Not completely, but some day when you think of Emilie, you will find pleasure in your memories."

"How do you know that, Louis? You sound so sure."

"Well, you remember that Maman is not my first mother, *non*? You remember Papa was married before?"

"I knew it," Marie-Claire said, "but I had forgotten."

"When my mother—Papa's first wife—died of the tuberculosis, I was only seven years old. I could not bear the pain of having lost her. For me, it was like there was a beast sitting on my chest who would not get off. Now, although I still think of my first mother whenever I smell biscuits or *tourtière* baking in the oven, I no longer feel the beast. He is gone. I feel instead the warmth of Maman's friendly smile."

Marie-Claire snuggled against her brother so he would wrap his arms around her. "It must be a terrible thing to lose your mother."

"It is terrible to lose anyone you love. And it does seem lately in our family that we barely begin to get over one loss when another follows."

"Louis, I really don't think I can take any more."

"I know."

"What if—?"

"Never mind. You must trust in God."

"But I did, and—"

"Shh," Louis said. "God will not cause you more pain here on earth than you are capable of bearing." He stroked Marie-Claire's long hair. "Does it help at all to know that we will all one day be reunited in Heaven, with God and with all those we miss?"

Marie-Claire sighed. "A little." She wriggled comfortably against her brother's chest. "Maybe in Heaven your first maman is Emilie's maman now."

"Maybe." For several minutes Louis held her without saying anything.

Feeling better, Marie-Claire climbed down from his lap and went back to her tidying.

CHAPTER N.º 4

When Maman returned from the market with a loaf of bread, a sack of lentils, and some vegetables for soup, Marie-Claire began to chop the carrots, still thinking about what Louis had said.

"Careful!" Maman scolded. "Is that how I taught you to hold a knife?"

Marie-Claire straightened her fingers, which had been curled almost under the knife blade.

"Honestly, Marie-Claire! If you do not learn to stop daydreaming, you will one day do yourself serious damage!"

"I was thinking, Maman, that perhaps the Linteaus should speak with the priest. He knows so many people, perhaps he would know of a place for them to go."

"Thanks to your kindness, Marie-Claire, they have a place to go. And one does not bother such an important man about matters that are not of spiritual significance. Madame and Monsieur Linteau know that, and so should you."

The carrots were all chopped, the soup was simmering on the wood stove, and Marie-Claire had settled down to some knitting when she heard Madame Linteau's familiar voice on the stairs.

"André, no. You must leave the snow outside."

Marie-Claire looked up from the scarf she was making for Papa and rolled her eyes. She had hoped to knit a few rows, at least, before the Linteau children came back with their constant demands.

Louis jumped up from the bench whose wobbly leg he was fixing. "Outside, yes. Come along, André. There is lots we can do with the snow outside."

"Me too," insisted Priscille.

"Let's go then." Louis herded the two children back down the stairs. Dear Louis.

Madame Linteau unbundled Michel and handed him to Marie-Claire, who quickly set her knitting aside. With a tremendous sigh, Madame Linteau plunked herself down on a chair by the stove.

Maman stirred the soup. "How did your search go this morning?"

"Not well, I'm afraid, for affordable clothing or for a place to live."

Michel grabbed a chunk of Marie-Claire's hair and gurgled.

"I don't know how Michel will cope when we do find a place," Madame Linteau said. "He has grown quite attached to your lovely daughter." She rose to help Marie-Claire disentangle her hair from the baby's fist. "Ah, *tu pue, mon petit.* Give him here, Marie-Claire, and I'll change his diaper."

"I don't mind," Marie-Claire said, digging deep to find her generosity. "You must be tired from all your searching, especially if you did not find anything."

"Thank you, Marie-Claire. You have a good heart." Madame Linteau sat down again. "I must say, we traipsed up and down quite a few streets this morning. One fellow I spoke to said that so many people have moved into this city in recent years, from the countryside and from overseas, it's a wonder anyone can find a roof."

Marie-Claire folded Michel's soiled diaper into a ball and wiped his rashy bottom. It surprised her to find that among all the irritations she still felt some sympathy for poor Madame Linteau and her family.

Madame Linteau said, "The best luck we have had in a long time, it seems, was running into you the day our house burned down. I don't know where we would be if you had not invited us to stay here."

Marie-Claire felt her face redden as she poked a pin into Michel's clean diaper. "I'm glad we have been able to help." There was a little truth to the words she spoke, but she wished there were more. How confusing it was to feel both sympathy and irritation with someone almost in the same instant.

When Monsieur Linteau came home from the textile factory that evening, a dark bruise marked the side of his face and his arm was in a sling. "One of the machines at work," he explained. "A belt broke and the flywheel caught me."

"Is your arm broken?" Madame Linteau asked. "Have you seen a doctor?"

"You know we have no money to pay a doctor," Monsieur Linteau said.

"I do not like the look of this," Maman said. Marie-Claire knew she was thinking of the weeks last spring when Papa had been unable to work.

As he was most evenings at dusk, Papa was out lighting gas lamps in the darkening streets. Although there was no danger in that part of a fireman's job, Marie-Claire wished suddenly that he would hurry home.

Monsieur Linteau rubbed his arm. "The wife of a chap at work examined me. She said nothing is broken, only badly bruised."

"Are you able to work, Guy?"

"Oh yes. It takes more than a few bruises to keep a Linteau down, *non*?"

A few bruises and a burned-down house. Oh, how Marie-Claire wished she liked this tough little family better.

CHAPTER N.º 5

School was out until after Noël and le jour de l'An. Marie-Claire and Lucille huddled against a raw wind as they made their way through the cold streets towards the market. Maman had forgotten, when she had shopped, that they were almost out of cheese. The Linteaus ate so much of it.

Passing between wagons loaded down with wares, Marie-Claire noticed an unfamiliar display of rope. "Isn't it odd," she said to Lucille, "that the rope is cut into such short pieces?"

"What good is rope in that condition?"

"Step right up, girls, if you want a good look."

"Why would we?" asked Lucille.

"Those be pieces of the very rope what hanged Louis Riel, that's why," the man boasted. "I can let you have one if you're interested, for a price."

Marie-Claire shuddered and pulled Lucille towards a cheese stall farther down the row. She pointed to a wheel of the least expensive cheese and held up her fingers to show the vendor how much she wanted.

The vendor cut off a chunk, weighed it, wrapped it in paper, and tied it with string. Marie-Claire paid him, counted her change carefully, then followed Lucille to find the oatmeal she was to buy for her maman.

When both girls had their packages, Marie-Claire said, "I'll see you later, okay? I have something else I want to do before I go home."

"Can I not come with you?"

"Please understand, Lucille. I need to do this by myself."

"Of course I understand," Lucille said. "Am I not your best friend?"

"Au revoir."

Clutching the paper-wrapped cheese, Marie-Claire paused at the foot of the church steps. Up three steps and down again she made footprints in the dusting of snow, then up four steps and down. When her footprints dotted all ten steps, she grabbed hold of the heavy door handle and pulled.

She was not sure when she had decided to approach the priest, or even when it had occurred to her that she could. Maybe the idea had started to grow yesterday.

Sitting in church she had remembered back to the fall when Maman was unwell. She'd thought then that it would be scary to talk to the priest.

But she had taken her courage in her hands, and had discovered the gentle concern in his voice that made her feel he would welcome her any time she was feeling troubled.

And she was troubled now—by her confused feelings about the Linteaus. In spite of feeling sorry for them, and being glad sometimes to be able to help a family in need, she most of all just wished they would go away.

Inside the church, it was very quiet. Only one other person was there, an older woman, kneeling in a pew near the front. Marie-Claire took a seat farther back. Wiggling her cold toes inside her shoes, she wondered where she would find the priest at a time when he wasn't conducting mass or hearing confessions.

Candles flickered in their holders. Through the stained glass, sunlight threw splotches of colour on the floor. Perhaps she did not really need to speak to the priest. Perhaps just being in church was all she needed to restore a sense of being right with the world.

Still, the priest might know of someone moving whose house could become a home for the Linteaus. Maman might not feel that finding houses was appropriate business to bring to a priest, but Marie-Claire's understanding of him was different. She slid from the pew and crept slowly up a side aisle, peeking in doors and mysterious little spaces leading off the main place of worship.

"Marie-Claire." It was like the voice of God behind her.

She turned.

"Are you looking for something?"

"For you, Father," Marie-Claire whispered. "I . . ." Again she took her courage in both hands, cleared her throat, and said, "May I speak to you about something?"

"Certainly, my child."

Marie-Claire returned with the priest to the pew at the back of the church, away from the woman praying.

"I have noticed," Father Brosseau said, "that your maman is back at church on Sundays."

Marie-Claire nodded.

"That is good. I take it the situation at home is also much improved?"

Marie-Claire nodded again.

"But something is troubling you still."

Marie-Claire found her voice and explained about the Linteau family. How it was that they had come to stay with the Laroche family, and their need for a home of their own.

"It is difficult to find lodging in this city at any time," Father Brosseau said, "and I am afraid the smallpox epidemic this year has made things even worse."

Marie-Claire's heart sank. He was going to tell her next, she was sure, that the Laroches must plan on keeping the Linteaus with them indefinitely.

"You are finding it difficult to share your home with strangers for such a long time," he said.

There was no use denying it. But would he not think her a selfish child if she admitted the truth of his observation?

"That is no cause for shame, Marie-Claire."

She felt a weight lift from her shoulders.

"Let me see what I can do to help the Linteaus find a more suitable living arrangement."

Marie-Claire nodded gratefully.

"More suitable for your family—and for the Linteaus."

Of course—and yet the realization surprised her—the crowded conditions had not been easy for them, either. She, at least, was in her own home.

"I have faith that something will turn up soon," the priest said. "In the meantime, remember to put your trust in God. Would you like me to pray with you now?"

Together, Marie-Claire and the priest bowed their heads.

CHAPTER N.º 6

Snow fell thick and fast as Marie-Claire skipped down the church steps. The prints her feet had made earlier had completely disappeared. At the bottom of the steps she lifted her face and opened her mouth. One by one, fat flakes landed on her tongue and melted there in cold little bursts. They settled on her long eyelashes, making the whole world look furry and light.

Praying with Father Brosseau had lifted her spirits. She was able to believe now that the Linteaus would have a new home soon, and she was relieved to find herself able to feel as glad for them at the prospect as for herself. She was able to let her mind wander to more pleasant things than her overcrowded home, where Maman was waiting for the block of cheese Marie-Claire had bought at the market.

Snow landed in starry clumps on the sleeves of her coat as she headed home. In not many days now, there would be lots of snow on the ground, and it would be time for the winter carnival. There would be sleigh races, horse races, and races on snowshoes, skates, and moccasins. There would be toboggan slides, lacrosse matches, music in the snowy streets, with skaters dancing, and visitors from faraway places—including, she hoped, her own Tante Thérèse and Oncle Henri—enjoying it all as they roamed through the city.

Best of all would be the ice palace. Right here in the square, where it had stood last winter. Marie-Claire stopped to imagine the big blocks of greenish ice sparkling in the sun, the corner turrets of the palace taller than her house, its middle tower taller still. It was like something in a fairy tale, only it was real. Last winter Maman had allowed her to go with Papa and Louis—Emilie was too small—to see it at night, when it was illuminated by a new kind of light that made the gas lamps that lit the streets seem almost dim. And as if seeing it all lit up had not been exciting enough, a group of snowshoers carrying torches and pretending to storm the palace had come down the mountain like a fiery snake slithering down a black hill. Trumpet blasts and the explosions of hundreds of Roman candles had filled the purple night sky.

Soon a new ice palace would be built. Soon the Linteaus would have a new home. And soon—in time for Christmas, maybe—her Tante Thérèse and Oncle Henri would visit with their new baby. Hoping Thérèse and Henri would stay long enough to see this winter's ice palace, Marie-Claire turned away from the empty square.

"Look out!" someone shouted.

There was a pounding of hooves.

"Attention!"

"Whoa! Whoa!"

Bearing down upon Marie-Claire was a runaway horse!

A carter ran to seize the horse's bridle. Marie-Claire spun out of the way. She slipped on the slick cobblestones. And down she fell. The horse's massive chest and heavy hooves loomed closer. The carriage wheels rattled close behind. But Marie-Claire couldn't move. Lying on the frozen street, Marie-Claire simply could not move.

"Where do you live?"

"Are you all right?"

"Are you able to sit up?"

"There is blood."

"Is there a doctor?"

"We must get her home."

"Where do you live?"

All around Marie-Claire, voices jumbled. She must be alive, she could hear them. But she could make no sense of the words being said. Were they speaking to her? So many people at once. She knew many English words, but she hurt so much. Too much to pay enough attention. Even the French carter, who had, it seemed, stopped the horse before the carriage rolled over her ... what was it he was saying? Why could she understand no one?

When she tried to sit up, the buildings around the square began to spin. She lay her cheek on the cold cobblestone.

"If she cannot tell us where she lives, we must take her to a hospital."

Hospital! That was a word she knew! It was in hospital that dear Emilie . . . Whoever these people were, she must not let them take her there. "No-o-o-o-o!"

Marie-Claire forced herself to sit up. "O-o-ow!" Her wrist. Her head. *"S'il vous plaît . . ."* She wanted to tell the strangers staring at her to *please* just take her home. But everything was swimming. She could not make the words come. Again she sank towards the ground. This time someone was behind her, and she sagged into his arms.

*When Marie-Claire regained conscious-*ness, she felt herself being jostled as if in a carriage. *Clip-clop-clip-clop-clip-clop.* She opened her eyes. She *was* in a carriage, and wrapped in fur.

She must be dreaming.

But her head would not throb so in a dream. In a dream, her wrist would not send pain shooting up her arm and down to her fingers.

"Surely, John, we can get our own doctor to tend to her?"

And in what kind of dream would she be lying with her head in the lap of an English-speaking woman?!

Marie-Claire shifted a little so she could see the English woman's face. It did not look unkind, even though on the side of her fur hat was the little snout of some animal. Marie-Claire felt the carriage slow and turn a corner. She felt its angle change. They were heading up a hill.

"Please, Madame," Marie-Claire managed to whisper, "no hospital."

"We are taking you home," the woman said. "Isn't that right, John?"

The man with the reins answered, "Yes, Winnifred."

Slowly Marie-Claire sat up. Outside the carriage, the street was wide and lined with trees. This was not the way home. *"Nous n'allons pas dans la bonne direction! Tournez-vous!"*

The woman named Winnifred laughed. "I don't understand a word you're saying, dear, but are you feeling at all better? Our doctor will come and tend to your injuries, but I do think a little colour is returning to your cheeks."

Doctor? A doctor would cost money. She had to get home. She had wasted too much time already, daydreaming at the square, and if her daydreaming were to cost her parents money, too . . . Oh, how very cross Maman would be!

Marie-Claire looked again out the window of the carriage. Fine stone houses sat far back from the street. Their grounds were big enough to hold several more houses, even with all their trees. Did the people in whose carriage she was riding live in a fine stone home like those they were passing? She had never seen this street before. How much farther were they going?

"We are dreadfully sorry for what happened," the English woman was saying. "Our horse has never run off like that before. How fortunate for all of us that the carter was able to stop him when he did. My dear girl, you might have been killed!"

Recalling the hooves and the wheels so close, Marie-Claire began to tremble, in spite of the warm fur spread over her. She held her sore arm close to her side.

The carriage turned up a broad driveway and stopped. Up the stone walls of the huge house grew masses of ivy—around its front door and all the way to its third-storey windows.

Marie-Claire tried to stand. Her knees wobbled. She had to allow the man named John to carry her into what was truly a mansion. Oh, Maman would not like her putting anyone to so much trouble, and especially such rich people as these.

Inside, the house was even more magnificent than out. There was an entrance hall. A six-flame chandelier hung from its ceiling. The first room past which she was carried had to be as big as her whole house. Beautiful carpets covered its floor. Paintings crammed its walls. Around the room were padded chairs and many tables cluttered with ornaments, candles, books. On one table sat a tree—a tree inside the house!—covered with little candles and ornaments. On its very top was a beautiful gold angel.

Before Marie-Claire had time to take in anything more, she was being carried up a grand staircase. So quiet this huge house was, with rugs muffling the sound of footsteps even on the stairs.

"Where shall I take her?" the man named John said.

"To Laura's room," his wife said. "Céleste has not yet cleaned the guest room. I will send Céleste up to assist her before the doctor arrives."

Guest room? A whole separate room just for guests?

Who is Laura? Marie-Claire wanted to ask. *Who is Céleste?*

But suddenly she felt dizzy again and could only close her eyes.

CHAPTER Nº 8

"*Bonjour. Je m'appelle Céleste. Comment t'appelle tu?*"

"*Je m'appelle* Marie-Claire."

What a comfort it was to hear someone speaking French. Céleste, it turned out, was a servant girl who worked for the wealthy family whose horse and carriage had almost run Marie-Claire down.

Marie-Claire winced as Céleste gently tugged her sleeve off over her sore wrist. Before there was time to feel embarrassed to be wearing only her undergarments in front of a stranger, Céleste

205

helped her into a nightgown, softer and thicker than any she had ever before felt against her skin.

"Cette chemise de nuit," Marie-Claire said, "does it belong to Laura?"

"*Oui.* Everything in this room is Laura's."

"But such a big bed . . . Has she no sisters?"

"No, she is an only child."

How lonely it must be, Marie-Claire thought, to sleep all alone in such a big bed, in such a big space. Much as André and Priscille sometimes drove her mad in the daytime, she was often glad of their presence in the dark of night.

"Céleste, can you tell me how to get back outside? I need to use the privy. Can you please come with me, too? I am still feeling shaky after my fall."

"I am happy to accompany you, but you need not go outside." Céleste helped Marie-Claire to her feet.

At the end of the hall, Marie-Claire thought her eyes would pop out of her head. In a room all on their own were the oddest-looking fixtures she had ever seen. A large white tub with claw-like feet and its very own taps. A wash basin attached by pipes to the wall and floor. And what seemed to be another basin lower down, with a box hanging on the wall above it.

"Do what you need to do there." Céleste indicated the lower basin. "In the toilet. Pull the cord above it when you are finished." She left Marie-Claire alone in the strange room.

At home Marie-Claire had often used a chamber pot at night, when it was too cold and dark to go outside, but it felt strange to be relieving herself inside the house in the daytime. Still, thank God for Céleste. How humiliating it would have been to have the wealthy English woman know how ignorant she was about such things as the in-the-house toilet.

When Marie-Claire was finished, she took hold of the cord Céleste had told her to pull. She gave it a little tug. Nothing happened. Nervous about breaking it, she tried again, yanking harder. This time a sudden sound of rushing water came from the tank above her head, and when she looked again into the toilet, her urine had vanished!

Céleste was waiting for her outside the door. "*Le médecin* will be here shortly. I will help you back to bed, then I must go and finish polishing the silver. Madame is expecting some guests for tea."

"My parents cannot afford to pay a doctor. Can you tell him please not to come?"

"Don't worry. Mr. Waterford will pay for the doctor's visit."

Alone in Laura's bed, with its plump pillows, Marie-Claire let her eyes travel the spacious room. On the tall windows hung curtains of the same pretty fabric as the cover under which she lay. In one corner, the door of a wardrobe was partly open. Inside it were hanging at least four dresses, each one a lovely shade of red or blue—Marie-Claire's favourite colours. Were they Laura's favourite colours, too?

Marie-Claire noticed on the wall a mirror fifty times as big as Papa's shaving mirror. She looked around the room for a picture of Jesus or the Virgin Mary, but there were none, and the room seemed suddenly very lonely.

As she was noticing a shelf on which sat a beautifully lifelike doll, Marie-Claire heard voices in the hall. One sounded, at first, like the awful doctor who had come to their house last summer, wanting to give her and Emilie a needle. But when the voices moved into the room, Marie-Claire saw that this doctor, with a black bag just like the other doctor's, had a blond moustache, not brown, and he did not have the shifty eyes of the one Maman had sent packing.

With long strips of gauze, the English doctor with the blond moustache tied a wooden splint to Marie-Claire's wrist and bandaged up the worst of her scrapes. She winced when his fingers examined her ankle, but he said it was only sprained, and if she put some ice on it she should have no trouble walking the next day. She had suffered quite a blow to the head, though, he said, which he would like to look at again in the morning.

"But I must go home," Marie-Claire said. "I bought some cheese. Where is my cheese?"

"You have had quite enough jostling about for today," the doctor said. "It truly would be best if you stayed here overnight."

"But Maman and Papa, and Louis—"

"Don't worry. Tell me where you live. I will stop by, tell them where you are, and suggest that someone come round tomorrow—I'll say midday—to fetch you back home. All right? In the meantime, rest well. The Waterfords will feed you, maybe let you have a warm bath. Just try to keep that splint out of the water. And I'll leave some more of this ointment to reapply to your scrapes. Does that sound good? Not a bad spot you've landed yourself in here, young lady, eh?"

Marie-Claire did not know whether to nod or shake her head. The thought of spending a whole night in this incredible house was almost too much to fathom. So quiet, so warm, and so luxurious. It would be strange to be away from her family, certainly, but in this bed that was so unbelievably soft . . . Céleste seemed quite nice, too . . . And tomorrow, facing Maman's anger and all the Linteaus filling her home, would come quickly enough.

Marie-Claire told the doctor where she lived, he said, "Good day," and again she was left alone.

Her attention wandered back to the shelf she had noticed earlier. On it sat several books, various ornaments, a wooden box, and a doll. Its dress was red and silky, like one of the dresses that hung in Laura's wardrobe. She wore knitted stockings on her legs and little boots on her tiny feet. So lifelike her face was, so blue her eyes, and her hair . . . was it possible?

When Marie-Claire was sure she was not too dizzy, she slipped from beneath the covers and limped across the carpet to where the doll sat. Between her fingers, she felt the doll's golden locks. Its hair was, as it seemed, real hair!

Marie-Claire touched her own head and tried to imagine a doll with such a thick, dark mop. Then she noticed, on part of the shelf she'd been unable to see from the bed, something that made her blink twice.

It was a little glass globe filled with water. Inside it stood a miniature palace with turrets on the corners and a tower in the middle—like the ice palace in the square! It was so beautiful she could not resist picking the globe up. And when she did, all around inside it—Marie-Claire could not believe her eyes—it began to snow! She watched as the snow drifted down and settled on the ground around the palace. Then she tipped the globe to start the snow falling again.

"Hello, poor little French girl. My name is Laura. And that's mine."

CHAPTER Nº 9

How dare this Laura call her poor little French girl. She might not be rich, but she wasn't poor, and she was every bit as tall. Yes, she was French, but why did this girl have to make it sound as if there were something *wrong* with being French? She was as awful as that snobby woman at the shop the other day.

"Lucky you not make me drop it," Marie-Claire said, trying her best to speak the language that was not her own, "come in like that."

"What do you mean? This is *my* room. And you are touching *my* things when I am not here."

"I . . ." Marie-Claire suddenly felt embarrassed, standing in Laura's room, in Laura's nightgown, holding Laura's snowy little palace, having rumpled Laura's bed. "I am sorry . . . it is only . . ." She handed the snow globe to Laura. "I never before see something like that."

Laura said, "My grandmother brought it to me as a souvenir of her travels in Europe. It's very valuable." She turned the globe over in her hand, watched the snow floating inside it, and smiled. Marie-Claire could see that this girl who had so many beautiful things was as enchanted with the palace in the globe as Marie-Claire was herself.

Laura replaced the lovely object on the shelf. "You should be in bed. Mother said you suffered quite a shock this afternoon."

"I am sorry they put me in your bed."

"I don't mind. Hurry. Let me cover you up. This room is getting chilly."

Marie-Claire found the room quite warm compared to her room at home, but she got back into the English girl's bed and let her pull the soft covers up around her shoulders. "Will you be sleeping here with me tonight?"

"Oh, no," Laura said, lighting a lamp. "Céleste will have the guest room ready for me before bedtime, or else Father will bring a cot down from the attic. There is no need for us to crowd into one bed."

An extra room, an extra cot. In this house and probably in many others on the hill. And yet below the hill . . .

Marie-Claire shifted her sore wrist closer to her body. Could she tell Laura she used to like sharing her bed with Emilie, that it was comforting to have someone close by as you slept? Even the Linteau children she did not mind, when they were sleeping.

But perhaps Laura would not understand. Perhaps she would think Marie-Claire must be poor if she did not have her own bed. What would she think if she knew also that her bed was not in its own separate room, as Laura's was, but sat in the main room of the house along with the table and chairs and the wood stove? In a room that also housed another whole family!

"What you are look at?"

"You had smallpox, didn't you."

"Yes, since many weeks."

"I can still see your spots. And you talk funny."

Angry tears rushed to Marie-Claire's eyes. Quickly she blinked them away. She knew she did not speak English well. She knew *la picotte* had left marks on her skin. But it was very rude of Laura to comment. "I wish you do not call me *poor little French girl,*" she stated firmly. "My name is Marie-Claire."

"I'm sorry. That is just what Mother called you. I heard her telling her guests at tea, 'Our carriage almost killed a poor little French girl this afternoon.' She was very upset." Laura sat on the edge of the bed. "You know, without your spots, you would be quite pretty."

Again, anger towards the English girl rose in Marie-Claire's heart, but she could only shrug. An awkward silence followed. Marie-Claire looked away from Laura, and when she again glanced in her direction, she caught Laura quickly pulling her eyes from Marie-Claire.

"To be honest," Laura said finally, "I am not in a position to criticize your English. I cannot speak any French at all."

"Most English people cannot."

"Will you forgive me for being unkind?"

Marie-Claire managed a small smile. After all, Laura *had* lent her a very nice nightgown.

Soon Céleste brought a tray and sent Laura downstairs to eat with her parents. "Are you two getting along all right?" she asked Marie-Claire.

"*Comme ci, comme ça.*"

"She is a lonely girl, Laura is."

Marie-Claire found herself telling Céleste all about Emilie, the games they used to play together and the stories she liked to hear. By the time she had finished eating the soft and salty vegetables on her plate, she had even told Céleste about the sad day when Emilie had died.

"You must miss your sister very much."

"I do." Marie-Claire pushed the tray from her knees. "At first I was unable even to say her name without crying."

Céleste removed the tray from the bed and wrapped her arms around Marie-Claire. "You are a brave girl."

Marie-Claire smiled. "Maman says that too."

"Say, would you like to take a bath before going to sleep?"

"I have taken a bath very recently," Marie-Claire said.

"In a bathtub like the Waterfords'?"

"No, never, but—"

"Come along. Let me run it for you." Céleste led Marie-Claire down the hall to the room with the toilet and bathtub. She whispered, "We'll put in some of Mrs. Waterford's bath flakes, shall we?"

"Bath flakes?"

"To make the water smell nice." Céleste closed the door behind them. "They makes pretty bubbles, too."

How wonderful it would be, Marie-Claire thought, to have a door at home that she could close. Just think how much knitting and other work she could get done if André and Priscille, and their maman, could not so easily interrupt her.

Marie-Claire stared wide-eyed as water gushed from the tap into the huge white tub. The level of the water, frothy with bubbles, rose up the sides. "Not too much," she said. "I am not used to such a deep bath."

"Ah, but you will like it, Marie-Claire, you'll see."

And like it she did! The water came right up to her waist. She had to be careful to keep her splint dry, but there was room enough in the tub to wriggle down till it covered her chest, and still her legs and feet were underwater too. She had not been in so much water since swimming in the pond at the farm of her grandparents, back before Grandmère had died and Grandpère had sold the farm and moved into Quebec City with his brother's family. That pond water had been cold. The water she sank into in this amazing bathtub was as warm as the water she heated on the wood stove at home. Céleste allowed Marie-Claire to soak until her fingers and toes were shrivelled like dried fruit.

Back in Laura's room and under the covers of Laura's bed, Marie-Claire chatted to Céleste in her own language about the crowded situation with the Linteaus.

When Laura came back to her room, she said, "Don't do that. I don't understand when you speak in French."

"Worry not," Céleste said in English. "We were not speaking about you." She picked up Marie-Claire's supper tray and said, *"Appelle-moi s'il y a quelquechose dont tu as besoin."*

Laura rolled her eyes. When Céleste had left, Laura said, "What did she say? Was she talking about me?"

Already Marie-Claire was missing the ease of being with someone who spoke her own language. "She say call her if I am need of something."

"I can get you what you need," Laura said. From the shelf she brought Marie-Claire one of her books. "Would you like to read for a little before going to sleep?"

Marie-Claire looked at the book. "I am able read only French."

"I'm sorry, I wasn't thinking." Laura put the book back on the shelf.

"Laura . . ." Marie-Claire said, trying the English name out on her tongue. "You want . . . I teach you speak something in French?"

Laura made a face, then shrugged. "Okay." She sat on the bed by Marie-Claire's feet.

"Mmm . . . *La française porte ma jolie chemise de nuit.*"

"What does it mean?"

"It mean, 'The French girl wear—is wearing— my pretty nightgown.'"

Laura giggled, then tried to repeat the French sentence, which made Marie-Claire start to giggle. Both girls were giggling when Céleste came in to tell them it was time to go to sleep.

CHAPTER N° 10

When Céleste opened the door to Louis the next day, Marie-Claire rushed into his arms as quickly as she was able.

"Marie-Claire," Louis said, "what is this I hear—from a doctor, no less—about you tangling with a horse and carriage?"

"Oh, Louis, I was so frightened." As Marie-Claire told her big brother of her adventure, she noticed that Céleste was watching him closely. "But I am fine now. The doctor said I should wear the splint for a few days, but otherwise, no damage. Just a few scrapes and bruises."

Louis asked Céleste to please pass along to her employers, who were not at home, a message of thanks from Marie-Claire's parents for the care they had provided their daughter.

"I will do that, yes," Céleste said, smiling.

"And thank you, too," Louis said.

"Marie-Claire," Laura said shyly, "will you come upstairs with me for a minute before you go?"

Less eager to leave the English home than she'd thought she would be yesterday, Marie-Claire looked to Louis.

"Go ahead," he said, glancing at Céleste. "I don't mind waiting."

Up in Laura's room, the English girl handed Marie-Claire a soft package. "Merry Christmas. I painted the pattern of angels on the paper myself."

A Christmas present? From an almost-stranger? Marie-Claire tried feeling what was inside. "What is it?"

"You wore it last night. My . . . *chemise den . . .*"

"*Chemise de nuit?*"

"*De nuit*. It is for you to keep."

Marie-Claire tried to hand it back. No one she knew exchanged such lavish gifts. And what would Maman say about an English girl giving her such a luxurious nightgown? So thick. With such pretty lace at the neck and wrists. "I cannot—"

"Please," Laura said. "I have many. I want you to have this one."

It seemed it would be rude to refuse it, so Marie-Claire said, "Thank you." She squeezed the package to her chest. *"Merci."*

Downstairs, Louis and Céleste appeared to be deep in conversation. Céleste helped Marie-Claire slide her good arm into the sleeve of her coat and wrapped the rest around the shoulder of the arm in the splint. She gave Marie-Claire a gentle hug goodbye.

"Some day," Louis whispered to Marie-Claire, "I hope Céleste will give me a hug like that."

The servant girl blushed, but she waved with Laura from one of the tall windows as Marie-Claire and Louis headed down the long driveway to the street.

"Louis, I cannot believe you said such a thing when Céleste could hear! Tell me, are you sweet on her?"

Louis smiled. "I have only just met her. But you know, I would like some day to have a wife and family, and I *am* almost twenty years old." Louis grabbed a handful of snow and threw it against the wall of one of the big banks on the corner of the busy street. "Some day . . . when I have a job that enables me to be a good provider."

"I would marry you if you were not my brother," Marie-Claire said.

"Do you not want to find yourself a wealthy man, now that you have seen inside one of their magnificent houses? Tell me, what was it like there?"

Marie-Claire told Louis about all the rooms in Laura's house, about her doll, her books, and the little palace in the snowy globe. She told him that her clothes had been washed while she lay in bed, in a special machine Céleste had told her about that did all the sloshing and wringing.

"I had a bath, Louis, in an enormous tub, and do you believe there was no need to heat the water on the stove? Hot water came right out of the taps—right into the tub! Enough to sink my whole body into. And when it was all over—*whoosh!*—down the pipe. Laura said she bathes twice a week—every week!"

"Would you want to bathe that often?"

"I never thought about it before, but perhaps, if it was as easy and as luxurious as that."

Marie-Claire and Louis turned onto the narrow road leading to their house.

After Laura's neighbourhood, where all the houses were set apart with broad lawns and gardens, everything here felt crowded. Dingy, too. Marie-Claire had never thought of her street that way before. And of course, home would be especially crowded with the Linteaus still there. Marie-Claire sighed.

"Louis, do you think English people and French people all go to the same Heaven?"

Louis looked down at Marie-Claire. "What makes you ask that?"

"Well, most English people have more money than most French people, right?"

"Yes."

"And not as many English people died of smallpox, right?"

"That is correct."

"Well, I wonder if . . . maybe they haven't earned Heaven as much—"

"Oh, Marie-Claire, you mustn't think that way. If God is measuring anything, I am sure it is not worldly wealth, or even how much someone has suffered. God is much more interested in how people live their lives, how they treat others."

"It was very good of the Waterfords to take me home instead of to a hospital."

"It was." Louis smiled. "And their servant girl is very nice also."

At the bottom of the narrow metal staircase leading up to her home, Marie-Claire stopped and dug her toe into a clump of snow. "Tell me, Louis, is Maman very angry with me?"

"I think so. She has been quite snappish since the doctor stopped by yesterday."

And for good reason, Marie-Claire thought. If she had been paying attention instead of daydreaming, she would not have had the accident. She would not have caused the rich English family such inconvenience—and a doctor's bill that she knew it would hurt Maman and Papa's pride to have had the Waterfords pay.

Marie-Claire remembered suddenly the cheese she was supposed to have brought home from the market. It must have been lost when she slipped and fell on the cobblestones. In the commotion, she had forgotten all about it. Perhaps, in front of the Linteaus, Maman would not scold her too harshly. Marie-Claire's stomach tightened as she climbed the narrow steps of her home and pushed open the door.

Maman was on her hands and knees scrubbing the floor. The back and forth of her hips and shoulders did not look happy. "Don't you be tracking in snow now," Maman said.

Marie-Claire looked quickly around. The Linteaus were not there to protect her from Maman's anger.

"I am sorry," Marie-Claire began.

Before she could go on, Maman got up quickly from her knees. "*Ma chérie,* it is you! I thought it was your Papa coming in here again with his snowy boots. Let me look at you. How are you? I am so glad you are home."

"You are not angry?"

"With those English people, I am angry, yes, for taking you to *their* home and *their* doctor. Do they think I am not capable of taking care of you myself, *hein*?"

"They wanted to bring me here," Marie-Claire assured her. "I remember someone saying to me over and over 'Where do you live?' But right away after the accident, I was unable to tell them. It was very frightening, Maman, I was so confused. The English lady, Mrs. Waterford—she said it was lucky I was not killed."

At that, Maman grabbed Marie-Claire up in her arms.

"Ow, ow!" Marie-Claire yelled.

Maman almost dropped her to the floor.

"Do not look so worried, Maman. It is just that my arm is still a little sore."

Maman laughed and then she cried, "*Ma petite,* I am so glad you are home." But when she noticed the package Marie-Claire was carrying, her eyes darkened. "What is this?"

"A Christmas present from the English girl, Laura. She lent me her nightgown, then said I could keep it."

A look crossed Maman's face that Marie-Claire did not quite understand.

"I am sorry, Maman, that I lost the cheese."

"The cheese?"

"That I bought at the market yesterday."

"Let us not worry ourselves about cheese today."

It dawned on Marie-Claire then how quiet the house was. "Where are the Linteaus?"

"They went off this morning with Father Brosseau. Tell me," Maman said abruptly, "are you able to scrub the rest of this floor with one arm in a sling? Or would you prefer to mix up a batch of biscuits to have with tonight's supper?"

CHAPTER N°. 12

It was tricky mixing biscuits with one hand, holding the bowl steady with her elbow, but at last the pan was in the oven. If she could manage biscuits, Marie-Claire decided, she could manage knitting—especially with Christmas less than two weeks away. She wanted Papa's scarf to be finished in time.

She had just managed to get into the rhythm of wedging one needle between her sore arm and her stomach and working the other needle with her good hand when Madame Linteau trudged through the door. Even André and

Priscille seemed subdued.

"It came to nothing," Madame Linteau said as Maman set a cup of tea down on the table in front of her. "Father Brosseau knew someone who knew someone, but in the end someone else heard sooner . . ."

"It is very discouraging," Maman said.

"We hate to be imposing on your family for so long."

"Nonsense. Your company has lifted my spirits."

"Father Brosseau will continue to keep his ear to the ground, he assured me."

"I wonder," Maman said, "how it is that he knew of your predicament."

Marie-Claire almost dropped a stitch. She kept her nose buried in her knitting.

Later that day, when Papa went out to light the gas lamps, Marie-Claire again had a chance to do some work on his scarf. She was more than a little surprised when Louis came home with a young woman. She was even more surprised a moment later, when she recognized her.

"Céleste!" A young man often courted a lady for several months before bringing her home to meet his parents. Her brother could not possibly know the Waterford's servant girl well enough already to be bringing her home.

"Bonjour, Marie-Claire. *Comment ça va?"*

When Maman looked confused, Louis introduced everyone all round.

"Enchantée," Céleste said politely, and then, "Madame Linteau, I hope you do not mind my putting my nose into your affairs, but Marie-Claire explained to me your situation . . ."

Marie-Claire glanced at Maman. Would she feel that Céleste was someone else she should not trouble with the Linteaus' business? It was not possible to read her expression.

"I have an aunt on Rue Papineau," Céleste began, "who is newly widowed. She does not want to move, but can afford to stay in her house only if someone comes to live with her."

"And there is room for all of us?" Madame Linteau asked.

"She has only one child, a little boy," Céleste said, "and room for your family can easily be managed. Would you like to come now to meet my aunt and see where she is living?"

When Monsieur Linteau came home from work, Madame Linteau greeted him with the good news. "We have found a new home, Guy. We can go there this very night."

"A new home? Where is it? How—?"

Madame Linteau explained.

"And Madame Gaugin has a boy," André said.

"I met him. His name is Georges. He is big, like Marie-Claire."

Priscille grabbed Marie-Claire around her neck. "I will miss you," she said.

"I will miss you, too," Marie-Claire said. The oddest thing, she realized, was that she meant it. Now that the Linteaus had at last found a home, and after her time at the quiet—*too* quiet—Waterford house, she realized how much she would miss having André and Priscille, and Monsieur and Madame Linteau, filling the house with their lively energy.

Since losing most of their belongings in the fire, the Linteaus had acquired little, so it did not take them long to get ready to go. They stayed for a last meal of biscuits and stew, bundled into their coats, then, after endless rounds of *merci, merci* and however-can-we-thank-you?, headed down the steep stairs to the back lane and out to the streets leading to their new home.

Marie-Claire leaned her head against a front window and watched them go. Priscille turned, looked up at the window, and waved. When the other Linteaus had waved their last goodbyes, Marie-Claire turned from the window and sat down on her bed.

From the parcel Laura had given her that morning, she untied the string and removed the paper. In the dim light of her home, she undressed and pulled the soft, thick nightgown over her head. She hugged Maman and Papa and Louis in turn, wishing each of them *bonne nuit.*

Stroking the fabric of the nightgown, Maman said, *"C'est bien moelleuse. Très luxuriante."*

Marie-Claire scurried to her bed and knelt beneath the picture of Jesus hanging beside it. "Thank you, God, for all you have provided. Please bless my family, the Linteau family, Madame Gaugin, and her son Georges. And now that you have found a home for the Linteaus, can you please make sure Tante Thérèse is strong enough to travel soon? I cannot wait to meet my new cousin!"

BOOK FOUR

Angels in Winter

CHAPTER N°1

Marie-Claire hugged her nightgown against her skin as she scampered down the stairs to the outhouse in the back lane. It was the warmest nightgown she had ever owned, but the wind still crept inside it and curled around her legs and neck. She should have taken time to grab the shawl from its hook by the door.

Inside the small wooden shack, Marie-Claire was protected from the wind and stopped shivering for long enough to lift her nightgown and do her business. But she was certainly not as warm as she had been when using the toilet inside the wealthy English girl's house. There the toilet sat in a special room with a bathtub and a sink, both with their taps full of warm water. In the outhouse, the wind found its way through cracks between the boards. As soon and as quickly as she could, Marie-Claire skittered across the frozen laneway, back to the house.

Maman had been up for some time and had already lit the fire. After warming herself at the wood stove, Marie-Claire pulled on her grey woollen dress. She thought again of Laura and wondered which of the many pretty dresses in her closet she would be wearing today. Staying at Laura's home, after her run-in with the Waterfords' horse, had been like visiting a different country. So large were the rooms, so luxurious the indoor plumbing. So many beautiful *things* there were everywhere—like the angel on the tree that Marie-Claire had glimpsed for only a moment.

"Can we get a Christmas tree this year, Maman?" Marie-Claire asked.

Maman laughed and tossed a slice of bread into the sizzling pan.

Marie-Claire wondered what Laura was doing now. Giving away her lovely nightgown had been very generous. Marie-Claire wished she could give Laura something in return. A Christmas present. But what?

She thought about it all day at school but still had no idea as Sister Chantal waved the girls out the door. *"Au revoir,"* the nun called out. *"Joyeux Noël."* There would be no more school now until January. No more adding and subtracting—too bad. No more memory work—*hourra!*

Without stopping to think about why she was not going home, Marie-Claire headed across the city instead of down the hill to her own street. Snow had fallen throughout the day, and many horses were now pulling sleighs instead of carriages. Marie-Claire kept well clear of their path. When she remembered how the Waterford horse had descended upon her, her heart still beat fast!

Perhaps, she thought, if she got more than one candy at New Year's, she could take Laura a piece. Marie-Claire skidded across an ice rink, her injured wrist tucked carefully inside her coat. As she zipped along, she dodged the people on real skates. Laura probably had real skates.

And Laura would probably receive lots of candy herself.

Starting up the hill, Marie-Claire slowed her steps. Everyone now was speaking English. The houses were large and so very far apart. How oddly out of place she felt in this neighbourhood, and yet at the same time she felt drawn to it.

Maybe a clothespin doll like the one she had made for Emilie last spring would make a nice present for Laura. Emilie had certainly loved hers.

But then, Emilie had been much younger than Laura and had never seen a doll like the one in Laura's room.

In front of Laura's house, Marie-Claire stopped. If she had a gift with her, she could knock on the door right now. Perhaps she would be invited inside. Perhaps Laura would ask her to stay and play. Behind which of the many windows were Laura's bedroom and her doll and her snow globe?

As she tried to figure it out, the front door opened. Wearing fancy hats and coats, Laura's parents stepped out to the fine carriage awaiting them.

Marie-Claire turned away and began to run.

What would a girl who owned a doll with real hair, a red silk dress, stockings, and shoes want with a clothespin dressed in a scrap of cloth? Marie-Claire ran until she had a stitch in her side, then kept on running. There was nothing a *poor little French girl* could give to a girl like Laura. Oh, how those words still stung.

Comfortably back near her own home, Marie-Claire slowed down to catch her breath. On only a few houses did she see the awful black-and-yellow SMALLPOX/LA PICOTTE notices that had hung in so many places through the summer and fall. It seemed, as Louis said, that the epidemic was almost over.

By the side of a church, as she walked along, Marie-Claire spotted a patch of untrampled snow. She looked around to make sure no nuns were nearby. What she was about to do, they would consider most unladylike.

Marie-Claire stepped from the walkway onto the fresh snow. Carefully, she turned and lay down flat on her back. So cold it was, the snow on her neck and on the bare wrist of her good arm. But after her long run, she didn't mind a bit. She gazed up at the blue sky that seemed to suggest anything was possible. Together and apart, together and apart, Marie-Claire swished her legs, at the same time sliding one arm up and down through the snow till her limbs tingled.

She stood up, brushed the snow from her clothing as best she could, and turned to admire her *étoile de mer*. Her starfish in the snow looked, she thought, rather like a lopsided angel. It reminded her of the angel on the tree at Laura's house.

There must be *something* nice she could give to Laura. If only she could think what it would be.

CHAPTER N.º 2

The next day Maman removed the splint from Marie-Claire's injured wrist. How wonderful it felt to swing her arm freely. Except for when she tried to bend her wrist too far, it didn't hurt at all now.

In preparation for the arrival of Tante Thérèse and Oncle Henri with their new baby, Marie-Claire polished the table while Maman took the braided rugs outside and shook them. She and Maman baked extra biscuits and readied the cradle for Angélique.

How lovely it would be to have a baby in the

house again. Of all the Linteau family who had stayed with the Laroches after their house had burned down, Marie-Claire missed Michel the most.

And yet, as she well knew, a baby's life could be so fragile. As if able to read her daughter's mind, Maman said, "Tante Thérèse writes in her letters that Angélique is a strong and healthy girl."

Marie-Claire was smoothing the cradle blanket in place when there was a knock at the door.

"Are they here yet?" It was her cousin Lucille and her little sister, Bernadette.

"Not yet," said Maman. "In fact, Marie-Claire, if you'd like to play outside before you go to meet their train, there is time."

Marie-Claire scrambled into her coat, and the girls took turns jumping from the steps into the growing piles of snow in the alleyway below.

"I was hoping," Lucille said, "that the Linteau family might stay with you a little longer."

"You were?"

"*Oui!* Then perhaps Tante Thérèse would come and stay at our house instead of at yours."

"Ah, but she is my maman's sister, *non*?"

"And my papa's sister also."

"Oh, but a brother and a sister is not the same thing as a sister and a sister."

"No," Lucille said, waiting for Bernadette to roll out of the way before jumping down into the snowbank, "but I wish I had a brother all the same."

"Yes, I am very lucky to have Louis." Marie-Claire did not say how much she wished she still had a sister.

Back up the steps she and her cousins ran. They jumped down again many times before Louis came out and said it was time to go to the train station. Lucille and Bernadette headed home.

Louis and Marie-Claire walked through the streets as quickly as the accumulating snow would allow, chatting along the way about the arrival of their relatives, about Céleste and when Louis would see her again, and about Marie-Claire's wish to give Laura a gift.

"You have been very busy knitting that scarf for Papa," Louis said. "Is there something you could make for this girl Laura?"

"I don't know. It is only a few days now until Christmas."

On one corner, a group of carollers stood singing. On another a street hawker cried out, "Tinware? Anyone with tinware to mend?"

A woman whose pot had a split handle came out of a nearby house. Marie-Claire joined a group of children gathered around the tinsmith's charcoal fire. She loved to watch him as he perched on his box, repairing things with his soldering iron and resin.

"You cannot watch for long this time, Marie-Claire," Louis said. "The train will soon be arriving."

Outside the station stood several horses, sleighs, and carriages. On the platform, many people were waiting for the train. So many people, coming or going.

"Just think," Louis said, "soon it will be possible to get on a train here in Montreal and travel clear across Canada to British Columbia."

To Marie-Claire, the city of Toronto, where Tante Thérèse and Oncle Henri lived now, seemed a whole world away. More country beyond that, she could hardly begin to imagine.

From far down the tracks came the long whistle of the train. Everyone turned in the direction from which it was coming. The ground beneath the platform began to vibrate. The whistle blew again, much louder and closer this time. Along with the rumble came the sound of what seemed to be a huge animal, breathing wheezily.

The monstrous bulk of the train soon filled the station. Its huge wheels and the long steel arms that moved with them chugged hypnotically along—slowing, slowly slowing, slower—mesmerizing Marie-Claire with their motion.

At last the train hissed to a stop, and Marie-Claire realized how tightly she had been clinging to her brother's arm. What would it be like, she wondered, to ride up inside this steel monster, high above the tracks and the world outside?

"Look! Here they are!"

Marie-Claire could not see her aunt and uncle among the crush of people but ran along behind Louis, holding tightly to the tail of his coat. Among the crowds of travellers and greeters, they called out, "Tante Thérèse! Oncle Henri!" then exchanged hugs and exclamations of delight at finding one another so quickly.

"How you have grown, Louis!" Tante Thérèse said. "You have become a man!"

Louis blushed but held himself tall.

"And how about this young lady?" Oncle Henri said. "She is even more beautiful than she was when we left for Toronto. Tell me, Marie-Claire, how is your maman doing now—and your papa?"

Allowing themselves to be swept out of the station with the moving crowds, they had little chance to look at the new baby, bundled and held close against Tante Thérèse's coat.

"Shall we take the streetcar back?" Louis suggested. "It is a long way to carry a baby and a suitcase, but I am not yet a rich enough man to suggest a cab ride."

Everyone laughed and agreed that a streetcar ride would be quite luxurious enough.

Settled in their seats, Tante Thérèse said to Marie-Claire, "Would you like to hold the baby?"

Angélique felt heavier than Marie-Claire expected her to. She had the cutest little button of a nose and her pink eyelids quivered. After all the commotion at the station, Marie-Claire could hardly believe the baby was still sleeping.

Riding the streetcar as it jerked along proved not much faster than walking. It made many stops, wherever passengers called out to be picked up or let off. Also, the snow was now drifting in huge piles, and the driver had to keep on stopping to wait while men with shovels dug out sections of track. Darkness began to fall over the city.

Papa would be out now with other firemen, each of them lighting the gas lamps in the streets near their fire stations. With the coming of night, the air grew colder, but with straw on the floor and horse blankets spread on their laps, Marie-Claire and the other riders were very comfortable on the streetcar. Just the same, when it again had to stop so that men could clear the track of snow, someone on the wooden bench behind Marie-Claire said they'd better soon replace the cars on this line with sleighs, as had already been done on the hillier north–south lines in the city.

With Angélique sleeping contentedly in her arms, Marie-Claire didn't mind how long the ride took. She felt already as if she had known this baby forever. As her aunt, uncle, and brother chatted about plans for the visit, Marie-Claire wished that Emilie could have met this lovely baby whose name was like the angels she had so adored.

In front of the church where they had to get off the streetcar, in the dim light cast by the gas lamps, a statue of an angel with outstretched wings watched protectively over a carved nativity scene. The Virgin Mary, with Josèph at her side, held *l'Enfant Jésus* in her arms. Snow settled lightly on the curve of the angel's wings.

In that moment, Marie-Claire knew what she would give to Laura.

CHAPTER N$\overset{o}{_{\cdot\cdot}}$ 3

"*We want to get off here,*" Louis said to the streetcar driver. The man pulled the reins, the horses stopped, and Marie-Claire passed Angélique back to Tante Thérèse.

The temperature fell as they walked the rest of the way home, but a cozy room and the smell of stew and fresh biscuits awaited them.

After supper, Tante Thérèse was quietly nursing Angélique in the corner, Maman was doing some mending, and the men were taking turns at arm-wrestling. "Maman," Marie-Claire said, "may I please use a block of soap to make something?"

Maman had an extra on the shelf in the pantry, Marie-Claire was sure.

"Are you planning to carve something?"

"Yes, but don't worry. I will be careful with the knife."

"I know you will. What are you planning to make?"

"An angel," Marie-Claire answered. She hesitated before adding, "For the English girl who gave me her nightgown."

"Oh? And how are you planning to get it to her?"

"I … I suppose I will take it to her."

Maman snipped off the wool with which she had been mending Papa's sock. "Ah, so you want an excuse to go back there, do you? Now that you have had a little taste of the fine comforts of the wealthy?"

Marie-Claire opened her mouth to argue, but the hard truth was that she did want to go back. She did want another taste of the luxuries in the Waterfords' mansion.

"You may have half a block of the soap," Maman said. "And please collect the bits and shavings as you work. Even small ones will be useful."

Louis cut the block of soap in half, and Marie-Claire settled near the wood stove to begin scraping. She had never carved soap before but had seen others do it. It didn't look any harder than cleaning fish, and she was very good at that now. She would save doing the wings until last, she decided, when she was used to the feel of how the knife and the soap worked together. She would start with the shape of the angel's skirt.

Tante Thérèse raised Angélique to her shoulder. "Who is the English girl you are making this for?" she asked.

By the time the whole story of Marie-Claire's encounter with the runaway horse and her stay at the mansion on the hill was told, the angel had a skirt and a head. Marie-Claire had forgotten to leave enough soap at the top for a halo but hoped she could solve that problem when the rest of the carving was finished.

When everyone began getting ready for bed, Marie-Claire begged to be allowed to stay up. "I have just one more wing to do. See?" With her hand around the chunk of uncarved wing, she held up the angel that was, almost magically it seemed, emerging from the block of soap.

"Isn't it beautiful," Tante Thérèse said. "I hope this Laura will appreciate what you are doing."

"She will," Marie-Claire said.

"Remember," Maman said, "how Emilie loved to hear stories about angels? She would have loved a little angel like that, wouldn't she?"

There was a moment's silence in the room as everyone paused to think of the little girl now with the angels in heaven. Then everyone said *bonne nuit* and left Marie-Claire with one burning candle by which to finish her soap angel.

It was hard getting the second wing to match the first. Rather than risk breaking it off by over-working it, Marie-Claire decided to leave one wing a little thicker than the other. She tried to fashion a halo for the angel from the scrapings, but in the end carved away a little of her hair instead, leaving only a slight suggestion of a halo.

By the time the angel was finished, the fire in the wood stove had gone out.

"Please, God," Marie-Claire whispered, holding the finished soap angel in the palm of her hand, "I hope you are taking excellent care of my little sister."

She shivered as she stepped into her nightgown. She blew out the candle and slipped quickly beneath her grey blanket, beside Tante Thérèse who was already asleep. In the cradle Angélique was making snuffling sounds. In different parts of the room, Louis and Oncle Henri were snoring in unison.

Marie-Claire shifted in her bed. Her nightgown was soft and warm against her skin. As she slept, angels swirled in her dreams. In the middle of them all stood Emilie, cupping the soap angel gently in her hands.

CHAPTER N⁰ 4

How strange it was to awake to the sound of a baby's cry. For months, mornings had been so quiet, then for weeks, there had been Michel Linteau's almost speech-like babblings. Now, in Marie-Claire's sleep-muddled mind, it was summer, Emilie was curled beside her in their bed, and Maman would be rising soon to feed Philippe.

When Marie-Claire opened her eyes, the space beside her in the bed was empty and cold. Patterns of frost were etched on the windows. The familiar claws of grief raked at her heart. The baby continued to cry.

When neither Tante Thérèse nor Maman appeared, Marie-Claire hurried across the cold floor and lifted Angélique from the cradle. The moment she did, the baby quieted, her eyes open wide. Marie-Claire smiled. It was hard to stay sad for long with a creature like this in the house.

"Are you surprised to see me?" Marie-Claire cooed. "Your maman is probably outside doing what I would say, from the feel of your soggy diaper, you have done right here. She will be back shortly," she continued, amused by how Angélique's eyes danced at the sound of her voice, "but would you like me to change you out of your wet things?"

Marie-Claire took a clean diaper from the small pile under the cradle. She laid Angélique on her bed, unfastened the pins, and dropped the heavy weight of wet cloth to the floor. Angélique waved her fists in the air and kicked her legs. Marie-Claire placed the fresh diaper under the baby's red little behind. "Such a pretty girl you are," she said. "And look how nice and fat you are growing."

Carefully Marie-Claire slipped her fingers between the diaper and the baby's skin as she jammed each pin through the thick flannel.

Tante Thérèse hurried in the door with a gust of cold wind, shaking snow from the bottom of her nightgown. "Thank you, Marie-Claire. If you would keep her a little longer, I will get some water heating on the stove so I can wash diapers this morning."

Tante Thérèse was filling the wash kettle and Marie-Claire was cradling Angélique in her arms when Maman emerged from her bedroom. Her tousled hair reminded Marie-Claire of the awful weeks after Emilie's passing, but recently Maman's spirits had been so much better. Picking up the soap carving from the table, Maman said, "Didn't this turn out beautifully? Laura is a lucky girl to be receiving such a gift."

With the angel tucked carefully in her pocket, Marie-Claire hurried through the streets. She hurried to keep herself warm and because Maman expected her help with the cooking that she and Tante Thérèse had been starting when Marie-Claire left. The family was preparing for the many gatherings that would take place between *Noël* and *le jour de l'An*.

When Marie-Claire reached Laura's neighbourhood, men in horse-drawn sleighs were delivering milk and bread right to the doors of the fine mansions. At the Waterfords' door, Marie-Claire took a deep breath and raised her hand to the big brass knocker.

"Bonjour," Céleste greeted her. "Come in quickly, Marie-Claire, out of the cold."

Marie-Claire was pleased that Céleste remembered her name. "*Bonjour,* Céleste. May I see Laura please? Is she at home?"

Up the grand staircase Céleste called, "You have a visitor, Laura. Shall I send her up to your room?"

"Yes, please."

Marie-Claire said, "With such wonderful smells coming from the kitchen, I thought Laura must be baking."

"Laura doesn't like to do kitchen chores," Céleste said. "But I'll bring you girls a plate of cookies shortly, shall I?"

"Oh, I did not mean—"

Céleste laughed. "Don't worry. I know you didn't. I can tell that your parents have brought you up well."

Laura closed the book she was reading and smiled. "Marie-Claire! I did not expect to see you again!"

"I bring *un cadeau* ... a present. For Christmas." Marie-Claire put her hand in her pocket. "I have no pretty paper to wrap, but here. I make it for you."

"What is it?"

Marie-Claire felt the smile fade from her face. *"C'est un ange,"* she said. "It is … an angel. I make it."

"Oh, yes, I see." Laura ran a finger over the carving. "It's kind of bumpy."

Marie-Claire wanted suddenly to run from the room, angry and ashamed at the same time. How could Laura be so rude? And what had she, Marie-Claire, been thinking, bringing a gift to someone who had so many lovely things—a doll with real hair, a palace in a snowy little globe, a shiny white toilet.… What did she think such a person would want with a lumpy bit of soap?

"It is lovely, too. Thank you," Laura said quickly. She kissed Marie-Claire on the cheek. "I especially like her wings and her little halo."

Feeling somewhat reassured, Marie-Claire said, "A halo very little. I think she is not the most … goodest of the angels." She giggled, nervous about her use of English and imagining what sort of naughtiness a small-haloed angel might get up to.

Laura giggled too, then turned the soap angel over in her hand. "I can't believe you made this yourself."

Marie-Claire's back straightened. "Yes, I made it! I—"

Laura assured her that she *did* believe her.

"But you say, *'I can't believe you.'* Does it not mean—?"

Laura shook her head. "It means only that I think you are very clever."

Sometimes trying to understand English was so confusing. But then, it was probably hard to learn any language well just by listening to people chatting in the streets and in the square.

"Say," Laura said, dropping the soap angel onto the bed, "Christmas is only two days away. Do you know what you're getting?"

"In my family, we give a gift at ... *le jour de l'An.*"

"Not at Christmas?"

"No." Marie-Claire held her thumb, said, "Christmas," then counted with her fingers till she'd indicated enough days to make a week. Holding that finger she said, *"Le jour de l'An."*

Laura nodded, but Marie-Claire wasn't sure she'd really understood.

"I'm getting new skates," Laura said.

"How you know?"

"Because that's what I asked for."

Marie-Claire's mind reeled. Laura didn't help in the kitchen because she didn't like to. She had only to ask and she would receive whatever she wanted. And she thought nothing, it seemed, of receiving a gift bigger than would fit in a stocking. Marie-Claire had always been delighted by whatever little gift the Baby Jesus left her—an orange, a banana, or a piece of barley sugar in the shape of an animal. How lucky Laura was to be getting skates!

Marie-Claire was just figuring out how to say that she must be getting home when Laura's mother appeared in the doorway. "Hello," she said, looking down her long nose. To Laura she said, "I'm afraid it's time for the little French girl to be going." Briskly she disappeared.

Marie-Claire felt her face flush. Why did being sent home feel so awful when she was planning to go already? The way Mrs. Waterford spoke— no "How are you? How is your arm? I hope it is feeling better"—it almost seemed as if Marie-Claire were not welcome here. But why? *Time for "the little French girl" to be going.* Was it because she was French? Or did it just sound that way?

Maybe it was fine for a French person to come into this grand home to work, or if Mrs. Waterford were feeling guilty about her horse almost running you down. Just don't think about coming here on a friendly basis.

"You don't have to go right away," Laura said.

"Yes," Marie-Claire said, "I do."

In one way she wanted to stay with Laura and her lovely things all morning. In another, she could not get out of there quickly enough.

"Before I go," she asked—wanting to stay was winning the battle inside her—"may I see, one time, some snow on your little palace?"

Laura took from the shelf the snow globe Marie-Claire had so admired on her first visit, after the accident. Laura turned the globe upside down and upright again. Around the walls of the castle, sparkly flakes drifted down.

Never before had Marie-Claire's stomach hurt from wanting a *thing*—a mere object—so badly. She longed to just grab it from Laura's hands and run.

When the snow had settled, Laura handed the globe to Marie-Claire. For a flickering instant Marie-Claire thought Laura might be handing it to her to keep, as she had her nightgown.

"You do it this time," Laura said.

The globe was heavy in Marie-Claire's hands, like a pound of butter. Oh, how she wished, as she turned it over, that it were hers!

Immediately she scolded herself for thinking such a covetous thought. But she just couldn't help it. The miniature palace scene was magical, almost as good as the real thing. When the snow had settled for a second time, Marie-Claire forced herself to hand the globe back to Laura.

And Laura replaced it on the shelf.

CHAPTER N° 5

On the day before Christmas, Marie- Claire sat in the back pew of the church, her head bowed. Which of her sins, she wondered, should she confess to the priest when her turn came? She had obeyed many of the Ten Commandments recently—honouring Maman and Papa, not using the Lord's name in vain. And she had certainly not killed anyone. But she had done less well with others—giving far more thought to the Ice Palace that she wanted so much to see built in the square again than to her prayers, for one thing. As for being vain and coveting her neighbour's belongings ... Marie-Claire sighed.

Wanting skates like those she'd seen people wearing on the river and at rinks seemed such a little sin now, with all she found herself wanting of late: a doll like the one Laura had; a snowy globe containing a little palace she could see and hold every day—even just one pretty dress like those hanging in Laura's wardrobe. Every time she went out in the cold to the outhouse, she remembered the shiny toilet right inside Laura's house and wished she had one of those, too. *And* a bathtub and basin with pipes full of wonderful hot water.

Marie-Claire pushed aside the red velvet curtain to the confessional, stepped inside the boxy little room, and knelt down before the blank wall. "Bless me, Father, for I have sinned. It has been three weeks since my last confession."

The priest slid back the panel in the wall between them, revealing only faintly his lined face in the pale light. "How have you sinned, my child?"

"I have coveted my neighbour's possessions. I think about the Ice Palace often. And, Father, one day I thought it would be fun to go on a toboggan slide."

"Are you truly sorry for your sins?"

"Yes, Father."

"Say five Hail Marys and you will be forgiven. And pray to God for holy thoughts."

Marie-Claire did as the priest said. Her heart lighter, she ran home to help Maman and Tante Thérèse prepare for the festivities soon to come. In spite of all they had already done, there was still pastry to roll, meat to grind for *tourtière,* and more biscuits to bake.

Maman gave Marie-Claire the job of whipping the cream for the special cake Papa so liked. Round and round in the heavy earthenware bowl, Marie-Claire flicked the whisk as fast as her arm would go. Her arm grew hot, and hotter, and more tired with every turn. When it felt as if it would fall off if she whisked a second longer, she simply *had* to take a rest. Her arm tingled as she let it dangle at her side.

But the cream looked just as thin as it had when she began. When she started to beat again, Maman said, "Keep the movement in your wrist. Remember, you are mixing two ingredients: the cream and the air."

Again Marie-Claire beat the cream, making good big but fast circles with the whisk. Gradually the cream began to thicken. She kept on beating, even as the muscles in her arm begged her to stop. Finally, when she again thought her arm would drop off if she tried to go on, the whipped cream began to form the pretty little peaks she was after. She put the bowl in the pantry, where it was cool enough in winter not to need ice in the icebox.

"May I lick the whisk and bowl, Maman?"

"*Oui, ma chérie, certainement*" Maman pulled a *tourtière* from the oven and put another stick in the wood stove.

Marie-Claire licked the whisk clean, then began to wipe the bowl with her finger. Other

Christmases, she and Emilie had kept a close eye on each other, making sure the other sister didn't get more than her share. Now that Marie-Claire could have all the bits of whipped cream for herself, they seemed, somehow, to taste not quite as special.

"Finished?" Maman said. "You might like to have a little sleep this afternoon. You will be up very late tonight."

"I'm not tired," Marie-Claire insisted. Who could sleep in the daytime anyway, right before the most wonderful night of the year?

"Well then," Maman said, "how would you like to take this little *tourtière* around to the widow Cornet? I invited her to join us tonight after mass, but she prefers to be alone. Poor dear, she has had a very hard year."

Marie-Claire smiled, proud that her maman, who had suffered such losses herself this year, was able to think of someone who had suffered more.

CHAPTER N° 6

Stars shone brightly in the crisp night sky. The cold air was still. Excited to get to the church, Marie-Claire and Lucille walked ahead of their families.

Marie-Claire said to her cousin, "The white cloud of your breath is almost like a halo around your head." She began to sing one of her favourite hymns. *"Je suis aux anges ..."*

Lucille laughed. "You have too much imagination, Marie-Claire. An angel I am not! Today, watching people on a toboggan run, I actually longed to be hurtling down it with them!"

"Oh, Lucille! You too?"

The girls lowered their voices as they entered the doors of the church. Before heading up the long aisle to their seats, they each dipped a hand in holy water and made the sign of the cross as they genuflected before it. Marie-Claire wondered if Laura was at her own church tonight.

For a month this church had been undecorated. Now, on Christmas Eve, the altar was covered with a gold-embroidered cloth, and the sanctuary was adorned with gold ornaments, candles, and bright metal flowers. Quiet chat filled the pews, along with the smell of incense and damp wool—until a lone strong voice began to sing *Minuit, chrétiens*. Marie-Claire was sure, right from the opening note, that inside her chest, her heart was vibrating with the music.

The whole church seemed to hum with excitement as the hymn was sung. A tall clergyman dressed in a long red robe embroidered with gold slowly entered the church, carrying a gold statue of the Virgin Mary on his shoulder. Behind him another clergyman carried a cross. Following him, at least a dozen men carried torches. Then came the boys of the choir, some in black robes, some in red, followed by candle-holders dressed all in purple. Finally came the moment Marie-Claire always liked best.

Someone carried in *L'Enfant Jésus* and laid Him in the manger. All around the church, real babies cooed and burbled. Marie-Claire looked at Maman. Was she struck by the extra power in the arrival of *L'Enfant* this Christmas too?

Maman turned at that moment from Papa to Marie-Claire and smiled. Marie-Claire slipped her hand into Maman's and smiled back.

When the first angel arrived carrying a bright star and singing the high, clear notes of the *Gloria,* Marie-Claire thought her heart would break from the beauty. All of tonight's ceremony was so familiar, and yet different somehow, as if all that the Laroches had survived this year— along with so many families here—had somehow made them even stronger and even more beloved children of God than they had been before.

After the shepherds arrived singing *Berger vois-tu là-bas,* to complete the tableau of the *crèche,* worshippers took communion, first the men and then the women. The choir sang more hymns, including Marie-Claire's favourites—*D'ou viens tu bergerer?, Il est né le divin enfant,* and *Les anges dans nos campagnes*—and she let the sweet strains of the music wash over her.

Louis gently shook Marie-Claire's shoulder. "Time to go home," he said, "for the wonderful meal you have been helping Maman and Tante Thérèse to prepare."

Marie-Claire rubbed her eyes. She must have dozed off during the long communion. "Lucille and her family are coming too, aren't they?"

"Of course."

Crunching home through the snow-clogged streets, Marie-Claire felt suddenly very hungry for *tourtière,* molasses biscuits, and special cake with whipped cream.

Late into the night, sounds of merriment filled the house as everyone celebrated Christmas. The baby, Angélique, slept peacefully through it all.

CHAPTER N°. 7

In the days following, toboggans flashed down the steep streets of Montreal. Where snow was lumpy, they leapt into the air and landed with a thud. All the toboggan runs made of wood were up and operating now too.

After what the priests had said about the sinfulness of tobogganing—especially for women— Marie-Claire found it a little shocking to see many young women hurtling down the runs, their legs flung impolitely in the air, the arms of men wrapped so publicly around their middles. She could certainly not imagine Maman or Tante

Thérèse doing such a thing, or even Céleste, who clung to Louis's sleeve and laughed with delight at the tobogganers.

All the same, it was hard to understand why God would want to punish people for enjoying themselves in this way. A visiting priest had said that was why smallpox had come and taken so many lives, but it made no sense. Emilie and other children who had died had never ridden a toboggan. It made no sense at all.

Hundreds of people were out enjoying the sun that shone brilliantly on the fresh snow—people in long coats and hats of beaver, moose, and seal and in short, hooded coats of chestnut-coloured wool, their waists tightly wound with fringed belts. There were stylish women with large bustles under their skirts, too, but Marie-Claire could not imagine wanting to look as if her *derrière* stuck out such a long way behind her.

At one of the many rinks that Marie-Claire, Louis, and Céleste strolled past, skaters flew by, their skate-blades hissing.

"Come skate with us, Marie-Claire," Céleste said, as she and Louis stepped onto the ice in their boots.

Usually Marie-Claire was happy to slide in her boots, one foot pushing forward, then the other. But noticing so many little girls out with their families, and missing Emilie, she did not feel like it today. Maybe if she had skates, she would feel more like skating. But she didn't, so she wandered instead across the square and plunked herself down on a bench that faced the area where the Ice Palace would soon be built.

Louis and Céleste came up behind her, breathless. "The ice on the rink is very fast. Are you sure you don't want to slide?"

Marie-Claire kicked the heel of her boot into the hard-packed snow. "I wish I had skates."

"Maybe someday you will," Céleste said.

Someday. Marie-Claire shrugged. "At least there is one thing I can have soon."

"What is that?"

"Soon the Ice Palace will be shining here again like diamonds in the sun. Louis, do you think Maman will allow me to come and see it with you at night, as she did last year?"

A worried expression froze for a brief instant on Louis's face before he managed to hide it.

"What is it? Louis?"

"I am afraid, Marie-Claire, that the city has decided … with all the disruption this year with smallpox … it …"

Céleste crouched down and folded her gloved hands around Marie-Claire's. "Your brother is trying to say that there will be no Ice Palace this year."

Louis began to explain why, but Marie-Claire did not care to hear. She did not want her brother's hand on her shoulder, trying to comfort her, or Céleste's sympathetic eyes upon her. She did not want the tears now stinging at the back of her own eyes. She began again to jab at the snow with her boot heel.

"Hello, Marie-Claire."

"Laura!"

"I have been watching you for a few minutes. You are sad today?"

Marie-Claire nodded. "A little." She did not feel like finding English words to explain but did not want to appear unfriendly. She smiled at Laura and noticed that the fur trim on her hat matched the muff into which Laura's hands were buried deep. Marie-Claire curled her own hands in tight balls inside her pockets.

"Can you come with me today to my house?" Laura said.

"Me?" She would be able to pee on that toilet again. Maybe Laura would again give her something, too. They could at least play together. They could be friends. But already feeling today like an old rag, could she bear to be around all of Laura's nice things? And—"Your mother? She ..."

"She won't mind. Please, come."

"May I, Louis?"

Marie-Claire was quick to notice that her soap carving stood small but proud on the night table beside Laura's bed.

"I love my little angel," the English girl said, picking it up. "I hold her every night when I'm saying my prayers."

Marie-Claire smiled, pleased to know that her gift was important to Laura. She was also pleased to know that Laura said prayers, even though she had no reminders of Jesus in her room.

Laura patted the space beside her on the edge of the bed. "Sit down, Marie-Claire. Tell me why you are sad."

"My brother, he say … this winter, there be no … *Palais de glace.*"

"That's too bad. The palace last winter was wonderful, wasn't it?" Laura placed her angel back on the night table. "But there will be other ice sculptures. Are you sure there is not something else bothering you?"

Marie-Claire squeezed her eyes shut for a moment. "My sister," she said. "I miss her."

Laura sat back and stared at Marie-Claire. "I did not know you had a sister."

"I think I tell you. Maybe I tell Céleste."

"Where has your sister gone?"

Marie-Claire struggled to tell Laura about the black wagon that had come when she and Emilie had smallpox, how only she had come home from the hospital where they were taken. She used such a jumble of English and French words that she wasn't sure how much Laura understood. But when Marie-Claire looked up, tears were spilling onto Laura's cheeks.

Laura took a lace-edged handkerchief from her pocket and wiped her eyes. After a few moments, she crossed the room to the shelf, picked up the snow globe, and placed it in Marie-Claire's hands.

Sitting on Laura's bed, Marie-Claire watched

the magical snow drifting around the palace. Laura said, "I would like you to keep it."

Marie-Claire thought she must have misunderstood, but the English girl went on, "I have so much, you ... Please, Marie-Claire, accept this, as a gift."

Her heart cried *Yes!* But she shook her head. She could not accept such a valuable gift. And yet, had she not badly wanted the snow globe every time she had seen it? "But you say before ... your grandmother—"

"She gave it to me, yes, but it is mine to do with as I wish. And I wish to give it to you."

Wicked she might be for coveting her neighbour's possessions, but Marie-Claire was delighted, too, to again be the beneficiary of Laura's generosity.

Together, the girls sat watching the flurry of snowflakes in the glass ball that felt like gold in Marie-Claire's hands. The snow settled again, on and around the miniature palace. It truly was a beautiful thing.

Laura said, "Maybe having this will take away a little of your sadness about the real Ice Palace."

"Yes," Marie-Claire forced herself to say. "Thank you." The beautiful snow globe seemed to have become even more beautiful for having been given by someone who was beginning to feel—how strange—like a friend.

CHAPTER N° 8

"First the nightgown, now this?" Maman, on her knees, wrung a wet rag over the bucket of water. "Is this what we have taught you is important?" She scrubbed a patch of floor, then sat back on her heels. "At least a person has *need* of a nightgown. But this ... this *colifichet?*"

"It's just that ... she likes me, Maman. And it's nice, that's all."

"Of course she likes you. What is not to like?" Maman resumed her scrubbing. Her hands were chapped and red. Wisps of hair clung to the perspiration at the side of her face. There was pride in the set of her jaw, even as she knelt by the bucket of dirty water.

"So, Maman," Marie-Claire said, "would you prefer that I return it?" She prayed that Maman would not say yes.

Maman rose from her knees, placed a hand in the small of her back, and straightened up. She picked up the bucket and took it outside to dump in the lane. When she came back inside, Marie-Claire, still holding the palace globe, said, "See, Maman, what happens when—?"

Without looking, Maman turned away to hang the wet rag by the wood stove. "Yes, I see."

Tears pricked the back of Marie-Claire's throat. She swallowed, set the globe on a windowsill, and said, "Where are my Tante Thérèse and Oncle Henri?"

"Thérèse and Henri are visiting some friends. Why? Are you hoping they will be more under-standing? The problem is not with wanting something, Marie-Claire. The problem is becom-ing too attached to the idea of getting it."

Maman was right. Marie-Claire did hope her aunt and uncle would be more taken with the globe than Maman seemed to be. "I just wondered."

"Well, there is no time to stand around wondering. I need your help to get ready for tonight."

By the time everything was on the stove or in the oven and people began to arrive, Maman was all smiles—for Tante Celine, Oncle Marc, and Lucille and Bernadette, for the Flauberts from downstairs, and for the Linteau family, the widow Gaugin and her son, Georges, with whom the Linteaus were now living. Again and again she cheerfully cried, *"Entrez! Donnez-moi vos manteaux!"* And when Georges noticed the snow globe on the windowsill, and Marie-Claire explained where it had come from, Maman did not seem to be upset anymore about her having it.

All evening long—after the older children had received a gift of candy and each of the younger children a simple wooden toy—everyone ate and told stories. Everyone wanted to hear from Thérèse and Henri what Toronto was like.

"Muddy, but lots of good jobs," Henri said.

"It is a little lonely," Thérèse said quietly. "But we are here now!"

Monsieur Flaubert played his fiddle, and there was much singing and laughter. Marie-Claire, Lucille, and Georges took turns bouncing the Linteau children on their knees. Later, after the young children had fallen asleep on Marie-Claire's bed, the older girls held the babies and rocked them. Lucille whispered, "This morning I heard Maman tell Papa that she is to have a new baby next summer."

Marie-Claire gasped. "Perhaps," she whispered back, "you will get the brother you have wished for."

Amid much merriment, Lucille raised the Linteau baby to her shoulder and patted his back. Marie-Claire cuddled Angélique close, enjoying the warm weight of the little body against her arm and chest. To Lucille she said, "Just think, someday we will be sitting together like this with babies of our own."

"I am going to have twelve," Lucille said. "How many will you?"

Marie-Claire thought for a moment. "Six would be a nice number."

"Will you feed them with a bottle, do you think? Or—" Lucille lowered her voice "—the way Tante Thérèse does?"

"That way would be much easier," Marie-Claire said, "if I am lucky enough to have lots of milk."

Both girls were taken suddenly with a fit of giggles. When the baby at Lucille's shoulder let out a loud burp, they laughed even more. Once they were able to bring themselves under control, they joined in the singing with great exuberance.

At midnight, everyone paused in their festive celebrating to kneel, except Papa. As the oldest person there, it was his responsibility to give the benediction for the New Year. Above each person, he traced a cross in the air and said, *"Que le bon Dieu te bénisse comme je te bénis."*

Looking around the room and thinking about how all these people had been part of her life this year, and she of theirs, Marie-Claire felt an almost overwhelming pride. They had been through so much. All of them. But they were strong people. Even in the face of injury, disease, fire, and death, they carried on. And so did she. She was one of them. Strong and proud and ready to face together whatever the New Year brought.

Again, the music started up, and Marie-Claire remembered the scarf she had finally finished. She brought it out from under her bed and wrapped it around Papa's neck.

"*Merci beaucoup,* my clever daughter!" Papa gave Marie-Claire big kisses on both cheeks.

Monsieur Flaubert played more fiddle, and everyone sang on into the night.

Gradually the music slowed. The voices that filled the room grew softer. Angélique was heavy with sleep in Marie-Claire's arms. When Oncle Henri said, "Shall I put one more log in the wood stove?" everyone agreed that no, it was time to be getting home—time for bed.

The families who weren't staying gathered their coats. After they'd left, and after much in and out to the privy in the back lane, the Laroche family and Tante Thérèse, Oncle Henri, and Angélique settled in their beds.

Marie-Claire listened through the wall to the peaceful sound of her parents saying the rosary. She heard the rustling of bed covers that signalled their getting ready to sleep. Across the room Oncle Henri began to snore. Outside the window, the moon shone brightly. On the windowsill—she had all but forgotten it was there—sat the snow globe she had brought home from Laura's house that day. Or, yesterday it would be now, for they had stayed up very late. It had been such a good party.

CHAPTER N° 9

The fire in the wood stove was crackling.
Outside the window, it was still dark. By the light
of a candle, Maman was quietly filling the kettle
from the bucket. Otherwise the house was still.

Marie-Claire watched Maman's familiar
movements. Something about them reminded
her of last night and how good it had felt to be
part of this family. Some mornings, it was she
herself who awoke early and did the chores
Maman was doing today. It felt good to know she
was as strong and as capable as Maman in similar
ways.

As Maman crossed the room toward the window, a little light from her candle caught the smooth glass of the snow globe on the sill and illuminated the castle inside. Marie-Claire lay as still as she could, not daring even to breathe, as Maman picked up the globe.

Maman shook it gently and watched the silvery snow swirling inside. "You are right, Marie-Claire, it is beautiful." So softly she spoke. She did not sound at all cross this morning.

"Yes," Marie-Claire whispered, wondering how Maman knew she was awake. "But I see—it makes you sad." She sat up, careful not to disturb Tante Thérèse. "Why?"

Maman sat on the edge of the already crowded bed. "A mother would like to be able to give her daughter all the beautiful things her heart might desire, whether she has need of them or not." She tucked a strand of Marie-Claire's hair behind her ear. "That's all."

Marie-Claire slipped her arms up inside Maman's shawl and hugged her fiercely.

"*Mon Dieu, ma fille!* So strong you are becoming!"

Marie-Claire looked up at Maman and smiled. The crinkly lines around her eyes, the silver strands in her dark hair, made her look quite beautiful in her own way. "We are strong people, Maman, eh?"

"Indeed we are. Tell me, strong daughter, would you like a cup of tea now, or would you like to stay in your bed for a little while?"

"Mmm … May I have a cup of tea in my bed?"

"*Quelle bonne idée, ma fille rusée!* Just be careful not to spill on your sleeping Tante Thérèse."

From the other side of the bed came a low, muffled voice. "You think I can sleep through all this chatter? How about a cup of tea for me too, Hélène?"

After breakfast, when the rest of the family was occupied, Marie-Claire wrapped the snow globe in a clean diaper, tucked it inside her coat, and said she was going out for some fresh air. When she had first seen the little treasure, she had wanted it more than anything she had ever wanted before—except to have her baby brothers and little sister back again. But Maman was right. She really did not need it, not like she needed a nightgown. Perhaps it would be enough to have seen it, to have held it, to know that such a thing existed. And to know that Maman agreed that it was a beautiful thing.

It *would* be enough, because she had seen the look in Maman's eyes even as she'd admired the lovely globe. Marie-Claire did not want anything so badly that she would be willing for Maman to be hurt every time she saw it.

Carrying her bundle carefully, she hurried through the quiet streets. It was too early for the tinsmith to be out, and shops on the main street were not yet open. The skating rink across from the square was empty. Facing the square where she had so often enjoyed remembering last year's Ice Palace, she sat down on a bench to rest.

It was where Laura had found her yesterday, before taking Marie-Claire to her beautiful home and giving her this generous gift. If she couldn't have the real palace, she could at least have this one. Marie-Claire felt proud of having made such a difficult decision. But perhaps … just one last look before returning it.

She removed the clean diaper in which the globe was wrapped. So smooth the cold glass. So magical the tiny flakes of snow drifting down through the water and settling on the little palace. Perhaps there was someplace other than the windowsill where she could keep it.

She was not going to keep it! How awful that her conviction to do the right thing could melt away so easily in the face of … what had Maman called it? *Un colifichet.* Before she confused herself further, Marie-Claire hurried up the hill to Laura's street.

CHAPTER N°. 10

*In the spacious entryway with the six-*flame chandelier overhead, Marie-Claire held out the snow globe to Laura. "I bring back."

"But …" Laura looked quite shocked. "I want you to have it."

"I do not need it now," she said, thrusting it into Laura's hands. But she suddenly was not at all sure she believed the words she spoke. The snow globe wasn't like a nightgown, it was true, but was it possible to need something, if only for its beauty?

"It was a gift, Marie-Claire. It made me happy, giving it to you."

As it had made Marie-Claire happy to give Laura the soap angel, she realized.

"And after you took it home," Laura continued, "it made me happy knowing it was yours now and thinking how much you would be enjoying it."

Marie-Claire's mind reeled. How bad she would have felt if Laura had refused *her* gift of the soap angel! But how could she enjoy having the snow globe if it made Maman sad to see it? If she *didn't* keep it, though, she would be making *Laura* sad! And oh, the little palace in the globe truly was a beautiful thing. Even Maman, who was so very practical about everything, thought so. Maman … *"Attend, je change d'avis!"*

"Pardon?"

Concentrating hard on her English, Marie-Claire said, "I would like … accept *encore* … your gift." She held out her hands. "May I?"

Smiling, Laura placed the globe back into Marie-Claire's hands. "I don't understand why you have changed your mind—again. But yes!"

"Merci, Laura. From Maman, also, *merci beaucoup."*

"Excuse me? What has your mother to do with this?" Clearly, Laura was as confused now as Marie-Claire had been a few moments ago.

"If you not mind," Marie-Claire said, "I share ... your beautiful gift ... with her. Yes?"

"Oh yes! Yes!" Laura smiled.

"She has need of the beauty, too."

"Please, Marie-Claire, since you are here, will you stay and play with me for a little while?"

Marie-Claire did not want to appear ungrateful for the invitation, but Maman would be expecting her soon to help with chores, and later today Tante Thérèse, Oncle Henri, and Angélique would be going back to Toronto on the train. She wanted to spend as much time with them as possible before they left. She shook her head. "I'm sorry. I can't."

"Then promise to come back another day? Some time when your brother comes for Céleste, perhaps?"

Marie-Claire liked Laura but suspected deep down that they could never be real friends— visiting in each other's homes and sharing heartaches and joys in the special way she and Lucille so often did. She leaned forward and kissed Laura fondly on both cheeks. *"Au revoir."*

Turning to go, Marie-Claire peeked into the big room off the entrance hall where the Christmas tree stood. She glanced up the grand staircase where she had been carried, not nearly as long ago as it seemed. The snow globe she held would always be, for her, a reminder of the special experience she'd had here, in this place that few in her community would ever see. She hoped the snow globe would come to have a special, happy meaning for Maman too.

As the door closed behind her, Marie-Claire had a sudden impulse. An idea for one last gift to leave for Laura. Mrs. Waterford probably wouldn't like it, but Marie-Claire wouldn't worry about that. Chances were, she would never see her again.

Carefully she set her bundle on the edge of the driveway and stepped across the smooth white grounds to a spot she hoped Laura would be able to see from her bedroom. Snow worked its way into the tops of Marie-Claire's boots, but it didn't matter. She dropped to her back in the snow, then together and apart, together and apart, she swished her legs, at the same time as she slid her two arms up and down through the snow. There would be nothing lopsided about *this* angel. Carefully she made her way back to the driveway and retrieved her package.

When she reached the end of the driveway, Marie-Claire paused for a last look back at the mansion that, two weeks ago, she would never in all her life have expected to enter. Then she turned and looked out across the city that stretched from the heights of Mount Royal down to the St. Lawrence River.

Someone was out there, paddling a canoe among the ice floes. Above all the buildings, between the paddler and where Marie-Claire stood, towered the tall steeples of the city's many churches. She could also make out the dome of the building not far from the market where she and Maman shopped. She knew that her home was among those huddled cozily together nearby.

Down the hill Marie-Claire ran and along the main street. Once across St. Laurent, she slowed down. When she passed the square, she felt somehow older than she had when she had sat there, so recently, longing for the reappearance of the Ice Palace. Of course, why wouldn't she feel older? It was now 1886. She would soon be eleven years old!

A few people were out now in the narrow streets made even more narrow by heaps of snow. A scattering of children built snow forts on some corners, and in open spaces others made slides and snowmen. Overhead, the sky was heavy with the promise of more snow.

"Are those arms?" Marie-Claire asked a girl who was sticking chunks of snow to the sides of her snowman.

"Wings," the girl answered. "It is an angel."

Of course it was. Marie-Claire should know angel wings when she saw them! She smiled as she hurried on.

Beside the fire station was a skating rink she had not noticed before. Had she been daydreaming again, or had Papa forgotten to tell her, as he usually did, that the firemen had made a new one?

No one was skating on the rink this morning, perhaps because of the brisk wind—although cold didn't often keep Montrealers indoors. Perhaps many were still sleeping after all of last night's festivities.

Marie-Claire did not want to linger. But who in the whole world could resist having a skating rink all to herself? Again, she set the gift from Laura carefully in a safe place among chunks of snow.

As Marie-Claire stepped onto the ice, fresh snow began to fall in silvery flakes from the grey dome of sky above her.

Over the smooth surface she slid, one foot pushing forward, then the other. She glided up and down the length of the rink, sheltered from the wind by the wall of the fire station. She stepped off the ice and went to a spot from which she could take a good run at it.

She paused to examine the snowflakes landing on her dark sleeve. How different each one was, and yet each one was beautiful in its own way.

Marie-Claire ran hard to the edge of the ice, planted her feet firmly, raised her arms straight in the air, and slid—right up the middle of the ice as smooth as glass all the way to the far end. The snow drifted down in lacy clumps and settled on her woollen shoulders, on her eyelashes, and on the ice and streets around her.

Legs pushing, arms pumping, she headed back down the rink for one last skate. Then, after retrieving the treasure that would be hers and Maman's, it truly was time to be getting home.

And Marie-Claire couldn't wait to get there.

ACKNOWLEDGEMENTS

I would like to thank the following for the parts they played in the development of this project: Leona Trainer for bringing to me the opportunity to contribute to the Our Canadian Girls series and for her supportive input; my partner, Peter Carver, for his support and patience during the period when I seemed to think of little but Montreal history, smallpox, and Marie-Claire's life; Barbara Berson for having the idea for the series and doing with Marie-Claire what good editors do; Barbara Greenwood, Gillian O'Reilly, Bill Freeman, and Maria Varvarikos for suggesting possible resources; Fred and Eunice Tees and Marie Louise Gay and David Homel for their special welcomes in Montreal; Suzanne Morin at the McCord Museum in Montreal for the time she took with my many questions; Victor Fleischer and Raymond Follows at the Musée des Pompiers Auxiliares for their time and interest in this project; le Centre d'Histoire de Montréal, le Musée du Fier Monde, la Bibliothèque Nationale du Québec, le Chateau Ramezay, le Musée de Marguerite Bourgeois, le Musée d'Hospitaliers de l'Hotel Dieu, Westmount Library in Montreal, and all the Montrealers who spoke French during my time in their city; the Toronto Public Library, and especially the staff at North

York Central; Michael Bliss, Bettina Bradbury, Herbert Ames, and Edgar Collard for their books and columns that were especially helpful in conducting my research; and Lena Coakley, Hadley Dyer, Paula Wing, and Wendy Lewis, whose feedback on the manuscript-in-progress was invaluable. I would like also to acknowledge the contributions of Cindy Cantor, Shelley Rea Hunter, Kevin Major, Janet Barclay, and Stephanie Carver for sharing their various areas of expertise.

1608
Samuel de
Champlain
establishes
the first
fortified
trading post
at Quebec.

1759
The British
defeat the
French in
the Battle
of the
Plains of
Abraham.

1812
The United
States
declares war
against
Canada.

1845
The expedition of
Sir John Franklin
to the Arctic ends
when the ship is
frozen in the pack
ice; the fate of its
crew remains a
mystery.

1869
Louis Riel
leads his
Métis
followers in
the Red
River
Rebellion.

1871
British
Columbia
joins
Canada.

1755
The British
expel the
entire French
population
of Acadia
(today's
Maritime
provinces),
sending
them into
exile.

1776
The 13
Colonies
revolt
against
Britain, and
the Loyalists
flee to
Canada.

1783
Rachel

1837
Calling for
responsible
government, the
Patriotes, following
Louis-Joseph
Papineau, rebel in
Lower Canada;
William Lyon
Mackenzie leads the
uprising in Upper
Canada.

1867
New
Brunswick,
Nova Scotia
and the United
Province of
Canada come
together in
Confederation
to form the
Dominion of
Canada.

1870
Manitoba joins
Canada. The
Northwest
Territories
become an
official
territory of
Canada.

Timeline

1885
At Craigellachie, British Columbia, the last spike is driven to complete the building of the Canadian Pacific Railway.

1898
The Yukon Territory becomes an official territory of Canada.

1914
Britain declares war on Germany, and Canada, because of its ties to Britain, is at war too.

1918
As a result of the Wartime Elections Act, the women of Canada are given the right to vote in federal elections.

1945
World War II ends conclusively with the dropping of atomic bombs on Hiroshima and Nagasaki.

1873
Prince Edward Island joins Canada.

1896
Gold is discovered on Bonanza Creek, a tributary of the Klondike River.

1905
Alberta and Saskatchewan join Canada.

1917
In the Halifax harbour, two ships collide, causing an explosion that leaves more than 1,600 dead and 9,000 injured.

1939
Canada declares war on Germany seven days after war is declared by Britain and France.

1949
Newfoundland, under the leadership of Joey Smallwood, joins Canada.

1896
Emily

1917
Penelope

1885
Claire